“A great read with just the right amount of steamy sexual tension and a HEA!”

—D. Yochum, Just The Write Touch, on Cadillac Cowboy

Also by Cynthia D'Alba

Whispering Springs, Texas

Texas Two Step: The Prequel (digital only)

Texas Two Step

Texas Tango

Texas Fandango

Texas Twist

Texas Bossa Nova

Texas Hustle

Texas Lullaby

Saddles and Soot

Texas Daze

Single Title Novellas

A Cowboy's Seduction

Texas Justice

Big Branch, Texas (Kindle Worlds)

****Kindle Format Only****

Cadillac Cowboy (Hell, Yeah!)

Texas Ranger Rescue (Brotherhood Protectors)

Texas Marine Mayhem (Brotherhood Protectors)

Praise for Cynthia D'Alba

"Highly recommend to all fans of hot cowboys, firefighters, and romance."

—Emily, Goodreads on Saddles and Soot

"Outstanding love story."

—Avid Reader, Amazon on *A Cowboy's Seduction*

"This book was fun and I loved every page of it."

—Connie, Goodreads on *A Cowboy's Seduction*

"This author does an amazing job of keeping readers on their toes while maintaining a natural flow to the story."

—RT Book Reviews on *Texas Hustle*

"Cynthia D'Alba's *Texas Fandango* from Samhain lets readers enjoy the sensual fun in the sun [...] This latest offering gives readers a sexy escape and a reason to seek out D'Alba's earlier titles."

—Library Journal Reviews on *Texas Fandango*

"[...] inclusions that stand out for all the right reasons is Cynthia D'Alba's clever *Backstage Pass*"

—Publisher's Weekly on *Backstage Pass* in *Cowboy Heat*

"*Texas Two Step* kept me on an emotional

roller coaster […] *Texas Two Step* is an emotionally charged romance, with well-developed characters and an engaging secondary cast. A quarter of the way into the book I added Ms. D'Alba to my auto-buys."

—5 Stars and Recommended Read, Guilty Pleasure Book Reviews on *Texas Two Step*

"I loved this book. The characters came alive. They had depth, interest and completeness. But more than the romance and sex which were great, there are connections with family and friends which makes this story so much more than a story about two people."

—Night Owl Romance 5 STARS! A TOP PICK *on Texas Bossa Nova*

"Wow, what an amazing romance novel. *Texas Lullaby* is an impassioned, well-written book with a genuine love story that took hold of my heart and soul from the very beginning."

—LJT, Amazon Reviews, on *Texas Lullaby*

"An emotional, complex and beautiful story of love and life and how it can all change in a heartbeat."

—DiDi, Guilty Pleasures Book Reviews on *Texas Lullaby*

"TEXAS LULLABY is a refreshing departure from the traditional romance plot in that it features an already committed couple."

—Tangled Hearts Book Reviews on *Texas Lullaby*

THE MONTGOMERY FAMILY TREE

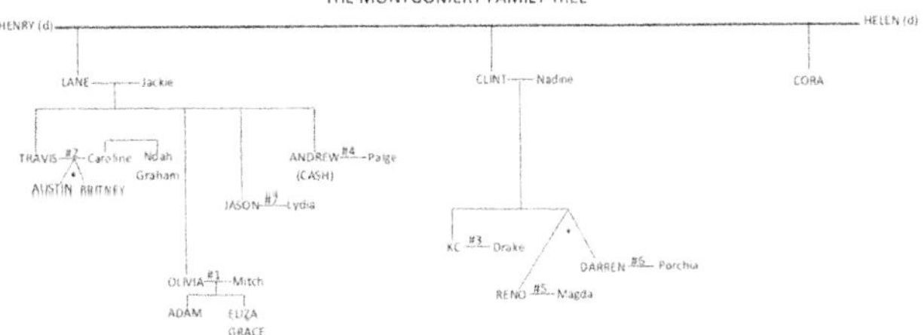

CAPITAL NAMES denote MONTGOMERY SURNAMES

- Denotes twins

#1 – Texas Two Step
#2 – Texas Tango
#3 – Texas Fandango
#4 – Texas Twist
#5 – Texas Bossa Nova
#6 – Texas Hustle
#7 Texas Lullaby

TEXAS TWIST

Whispering Springs, Texas

CYNTHIA D'ALBA

TEXAS TWIST

By Cynthia D'Alba

Second Edition 2017

Print ISBN: 978-1-946899-12-5

Digital ISBN: 978-1-946899-10-1

Cover Artist: Elle James

Editor: Heidi (Moore) Shoham

Dedication

With every book, I get the chance to recognize people who have contributed in some way to the book and to my success. I struggle with this because there are usually so many. As always, critique partners Angela Campbell, Sandra Jones and Pamela Hearon provided immeasurable help with their edits and suggestions.

Thank you to my parents who always told me that I can do anything and then gave me the support to do just that.

Thank you to my nitpicky editor, Heidi Moore. I moan, shriek and brood through my edits, but you never fail to improve my writing and my story. I adore you!

And of course my darling husband, Phil, who goes fishing during edits so I can have a quiet house. I love you.

Thank you to Buster Gilliam for the use of your name for Cash's new dog. You are the world's best electrician.

And finally, a huge debt of gratitude to D'Alba Diamonds, my street team. These ladies are always ready to give title suggestions, reviews and help with any promotion for my books, not to mention the great jokes, opinions and advice they offer so freely. Life would be harder without them. Lisa Boggs, Laura Mixon Bow, Tanya Brown, Sandra Butler, Nancy Davidson, Paula Farrell, Nita Flannigan, Paige Gregory, Sandy Haber, Kelly Lynders Haddox, Bette Hansen, Shadow Kohler, Sue Lopp, Karen McDonald, Lori Meehan, Dawn Morris, Michelle Oxrider, Melanie Pashon, Maria Proctor, Jill Purinton, Tracey Reid, Tina Reiter, Brenda Rumsey, Jessica Sheehan, Ruth Smithson, Kimberly Stripling, Veronica Vasquez, Susie Wilson Williams and Delene Yochum.

And last, but so very important, thank you to Kim Rocha. Without Kim, D'Alba Diamonds would not exist. I love you all. Thank you from the bottom of my heart for all you do.

And, as I review and revise this book, thanks to you reader for getting this far in the dedication!

Prologue

Late October

"Let me see the ring."

KC Montgomery held out her left hand. Olivia grabbed KC's fingers and pulled her closer to examine the three-carat emerald-cut diamond. Under Olivia's kitchen lights, colors from the stone zinged around the room.

"Wow." Olivia looked at Caroline, her newest sister-in-law. "I'm impressed."

"It's beautiful, KC," Caroline said and then hugged her friend. "I am so happy for you and Drake. I'm looking forward to the wedding."

A voice from the front door shouted, "Pizza delivery."

"Finally," Olivia said. "I'm starving."

Jason Montgomery and Lydia Henson, his fiancée, walked in carrying six large pizza boxes.

"Think you got enough pizza there, bro?" Travis asked.

"Maybe," Jason replied, stacking the boxes on the kitchen island. "I've seen you eat. Leave some for the rest of us."

"Hey, guys. You might want to check the time." Olivia pointed to the clock. "Cash should be riding soon."

The group got drinks, plates loaded with pizza and a stack of napkins and headed for the Landrys' television room, better known as the Man Cave.

"Okay, ladies," Mitch said as everyone found seats in front of his eighty-inch television. "We men are sharing our space with you tonight, but don't get any ideas about book clubs or chick flicks in here."

The four women exchanged eye-rolls and then laughed.

"What time does Cash ride?" Caroline asked.

"Soon," Travis answered.

Cash Montgomery, the youngest brother of Travis, Jason and Olivia, was on track to win the Professional Bull Riders world championship for a third consecutive time, a feat rarely seen at this level of competition.

"Glad Mom and Dad got to go out." Jason wiped his mouth. "Cash says this will be his last year, win or lose, but with the way he's riding, I'm thinking he'll go out a winner."

"I hope so," Olivia said. "Mom hates these rides. Says she watches like this." Olivia covered her eyes with her hands and then peeked between her fingers. That got a chuckle from the group.

"Who'd he draw this round?" Drake asked.

"Bad Bob."

The Montgomery clan and Drake moaned.

"What?" Caroline asked.

Travis pulled her onto his lap. "Bad Bob's earned his name. Ranks up there with some of the greats. Asteroid. Bushwacker. Devil's Child. He'll be tough."

"But Cash can ride him, right?" Caroline asked.

"My little brother can ride anything," Olivia said.

"Hey. Turn up the volume." Lydia pointed to the screen. "Isn't that Cash?"

Eight pairs of eyes focused on the television as the youngest Montgomery strutted down a hallway.

"And this is defending champion, Cash Montgomery," the first commentator said.

"He's got a rough ride ahead of him," the second announcer replied.

"He's young and he's tough. I think he's looking good for another big win, Ty."

"Tell me about the bull he's pulled for tonight."

"Bad Bob is at the top of his game, but he has a couple of signature moves that the cowboys watch for. He always swings to the right. Never to the left so—"

Mitch muted the sound. "Just think. One day the announcers could be talking about one of our bulls." He and Cash had recently gone into partnership to breed and raise bulls for the professional rodeo.

"Think it'll be easier to watch one of our bulls instead of my little brother?" Olivia asked with an arched eyebrow.

Mitch snorted. "Probably not." He glanced at the television. "He's up."

Mitch unmuted the sound. The room fell silent as they watched Cash Montgomery climb on the back of a fifteen-hundred-pound bull and begin setting the rope in his hand.

"Your brother is nuts," Caroline said. "No sane person would do that."

"Who said anything about Cash being sane?" Olivia replied.

The announcers on television kept up the commentary, talking about Cash's wins, his previous scores, his outstanding talent and his long-term potential.

As Cash raised his hand to indicate he was ready, the tension in the Landry house rose to palpable levels. Breaths were sucked in as the eight adults got ready to watch.

The gray Brahma bull shot through the gate like a missile. All four feet left the ground when he jumped and tried to dislodge Cash from his back. The bull's feet barely touched the dirt surface before he was in the air again, swinging to the left. Cash flew off and was trapped between the massive animal and a metal gate. Bad Bob slammed Cash against the gate again before he could get his hand rope released. The bull pummeled Cash again and threw him to the arena floor. Bad Bob leapt one more time, landing on Cash's legs. Then he ran up Cash's chest and finished with a kick to the head.

The bullfighters were waving and yelling at Bad

Bob, trying to draw his attention away from the unmoving body lying in the arena dirt. Bad Bob saw the open exit gate, raced through it and down the chute away from the crowd and toward his pen.

The stunned silence of the rodeo crowd matched the stunned silence watching at home.

Mitch picked up his phone and made a call. "Carl? Gas up my plane and make sure it's ready to go. We'll be at the airport within an hour."

Travis stood. "I'm going too."

"So am I." Jason said, rising from the couch.

"You guys go do what you need to do. I'll stay here and take care of this end," Drake said.

"The plane's only a four-seater," Olivia said. "I'll stay here with Adam until we know more. I can take a flight out later. Take Lydia or Caroline with you. You need someone who can understand medically what's going on."

"Take Caroline," Lydia said. "She's got a lot more experience in trauma than I do."

"Don't worry about the office," KC said to Jason. "Margaret and I can handle anything that comes up."

"Caroline and I will head to our house to pack a bag. John Webster can handle everything at the ranch." Travis grabbed Caroline's hand and headed for the door.

"What about clothes for you?" Lydia asked Jason.

"He can wear mine," Travis said over his shoulder. "Or hell, he can buy some. Let's go."

Tears filled Olivia's eyes as she hugged her husband. "Call me."

"I will. The second we know anything."

"Call me before then. I need to hear even if the news is that we don't know anything."

Less than an hour later, three trucks pulled in at the small Whispering Springs Municipal Airport. While Mitch did his pre-flight check, Travis and Jason loaded small suitcases into the plane's belly. Then Travis, Caroline and Jason climbed on Mitch's plane and waved goodbye to their family and friends as they flew to Las Vegas.

Chapter One

Six months later

It was nearly midnight when Paige Ryan wheeled into Leo's Bar and Grill's almost-empty parking lot. She took the spot by the rear door and climbed out. The night air was a cool respite from the late April day's heat. She let herself in, and after a quick wave to the night cook finishing the kitchen clean-up, she made her way to the bar.

"Okay, I'm here," she said and slipped under the counter door. "Would have been here ten minutes ago, but I'm still packing my stuff into moving boxes." She tied an apron around her waist.

Her brother, Leo Elroy Mabee, the establishment's owner, finished drawing a beer before turning toward her. "Thanks for coming on short notice. Tonight's business has died down so you should have an easy close." He pulled another beer mug from below the bar. "You hear from Uncle James again today?"

She leaned against the counter, crossing one foot over the other. "Yup. He'll be home in a couple of weeks. I still can't believe he got married. Can you?"

Her brother shook his head. "Not really. Not after all these years. Have you decided where you're going to move? You can come stay with me, you know."

She laughed. "Thanks, but no thanks. I couldn't take all the revolving women in your life. But not to worry. Found a place. It'll take me a couple of days to get it in tip-top shape, but I'll be able to move in pretty fast. Maybe even tomorrow. At the least, I'll be gone when James and his bride get home. I figure newlyweds need their private space. But damn, I'm going to miss his pool. Oh, and his huge television. And his kitchen." She sighed. "I'll really miss his kitchen."

Leo chuckled. "Living in his house spoiled you, did it?" He pulled another beer and handed it to a waitress.

"You have no idea." She gave her brother a sideways glance. "Do you still miss Mom and Dad as much as I do?"

Leo's gaze met hers. "Unbelievably so. What brought this on?"

"I don't know. Maybe Uncle James finally coming home. Life moving on. I know it's been ten months since they died, but I still sometimes forget they're gone. Today, I picked up the phone to call Mom. I wanted to tell her about my new house and ask her advice on what to get Uncle James for a wedding present." She quirked up the side of her mouth. "He has everything. I kid you not."

"It was good you came to stay with James when Mom died. I think your being here helped him deal with their deaths."

"Maybe, but…" she shrugged.

"Where you moving?" he asked, mixing a Tom Collins for a waiting customer.

"Caroline Graham has an old farm house she's going to let me rent for a while."

"Oh, you mean the old Fitzgerald place?" He slid the drink into the hands of a young, attractive blonde.

"Yeah. You know it?"

"Not really. I remember old man Fitzgerald. Everybody around here was surprised to find out Dr. Graham was kin. But it'll be a good place for you to land for a while." Leo wiped his hands on a towel hanging from his waist. "I'm glad you're getting out of this bar. You were wasting your education here."

Paige shoved at his shoulder. "I loved being with you, bro."

He smiled. "Maybe, but with a bachelor degree in psychology and another in nursing, you should be doing more than slinging drinks."

"I'll miss seeing your ugly mug every day."

He elbowed her ribs, making her giggle. "So, work on Monday at Whispering Springs Medical Clinic. You excited?"

She shrugged. "More nervous, I think. Been a while since I actually used my nursing education."

"You'll do fine." He checked his watch. "I need to get moving." He pulled a bottled beer from the cooler and used it to point to a booth in the corner. "This is *his* last one. Keep an eye on him. You'll need to call a cab or one of his brothers to pick him up."

He twisted the top off the beer and handed the bottle to Sally, the waitress. She carried the fresh beer to the man in the corner. He took the bottle and downed the beer in a long gulp before resting his head on the table.

Paige studied the drunk in the booth. Her heart cried to see how far he'd fallen. She'd know him anywhere, not that he'd remember her. Andrew Lane Montgomery, aka Cash Montgomery, World Professional Bull Riding Champion two years in a row until his tragic accident last October. She must have seen every one of his rides over the years, including the last one. Her stomach clenched at the memory.

Cash had been called invincible. She thought he'd probably believed it too until Bad Bob. That bull hated cowboys and made sure they paid for being on his back. Cash had paid all right. Broken left leg, fractured ribs, punctured lung and spleen, broken arms and a major concussion. He was damn lucky to be alive, but looking at him slumped in the back booth, a healthy collection of beer bottles littering his table, he appeared to be attempting death by alcohol poisoning.

"Why'd you let him drink so much? You should have stopped him hours ago."

"First—" Leo said, ticking off the points on his fingers, "—I'm not his momma. Second, he's over twenty-one. And third, I took his truck keys." He opened the door on a valet cabinet and pointed to a set of keys. "They're here. He can't have them back tonight. He knows that." He slammed the cabinet door. "On second thought, let him sleep it off in the drunk room upstairs. He certainly wouldn't be the first Montgomery to use that room."

"And don't call Travis or Jason?"

He nodded. "Right. If he's still up there when I get here at noon, I'll call someone. Okay, I'm gone. Thanks again for closing. I owe you one."

"Wait. You never told me what the urgent crisis was that dictated my getting out of bed and driving here in the middle of the night."

He grinned. "Nope. I never did." And with that, he hurried out the back door.

Smiling and shaking her head, she picked up the bar rag Leo had dropped and folded it. "Has to be a woman," she muttered. Knowing her brother's reputation as a love-'em-and-leave-'em guy, she felt a moment of pity for the female entertaining him tonight…and she was sure it was a woman who'd called him away. But then that wasn't her problem.

"What'd you say?" Donald, the night bartender, asked.

"Nothing." She let her gaze sweep the room. Not a lot of customers, but not surprising for a late Wednesday night in the Bible belt.

Now tomorrow night? This place will still be hopping at midnight.

For the next couple of hours, Sally circled the floor for the few customers remaining. Paige or Donald pulled beers or made drinks as needed. Since it was slow, she cleaned the liquor shelves all the while watching Cash Montgomery in the mirror. His hair was too long. His body was way too thin, almost emaciated-looking. Oh, the muscles were still there. She could see those when he shifted in the booth. He'd always been bigger than life in her eyes, but right now he looked like he needed a lot more food and a lot less alcohol in his diet.

About ten minutes before closing, she pulled a tray from beneath the bar and headed out to clear the empties off Cash's table.

"I can do that," Sally said, hurrying over.

Paige shook her head. "Don't worry about it. I thought maybe we could get ahead of the closing clean-up."

"You have his keys, right? Leo said he'd taken them."

Sally's cheeks flushed at the mention of Leo's name. Had Sally been another one of her brother's hit-and-run affairs? Paige hoped not. She liked the young woman and would hate a love affair gone wrong to run her off. Good waitresses were hard to find, and Sally was one of the best.

"I've got them. Leo said to put him upstairs for tonight. Once we clear out the customers, Donald and I can take care of him."

Whatever Sally was going to say was drowned out by a long gong from the bar. "Last call," Donald shouted. "Closing in ten minutes."

"Guess I'd better make one last round." Sally made her way from table to table, closing bar tabs or delivering one last drink.

Paige picked up five empty beer bottles from Cash's table and headed back to the bar, pausing to dump them in the trash on her way.

The room's dim lighting encouraged the bar patrons to hang around and keep drinking. However, as soon as Paige flicked on the overhead lights, customers collected their personal belongings and made for the exit.

Sally and Donald began setting the chairs upside down on the tables to clear the floor for mopping. Paige cleared the cash register and took the cash into Leo's office to secure tonight's receipts in his safe.

When she reentered the bar, Cash was snoring, Sally was running a mop around the floor and Donald was loading the last tray of glasses into the washer.

"About done?" Paige asked.

"I am," Sally said, taking a final swipe with the mop. After returning it to the janitor closet, she yawned and stretched. "I'm sleeping 'til noon tomorrow. I'm out of here."

"Hold on," Donald said, tucking a Smith and Wesson forty-five into his pocket. "I'll walk you out."

They headed out and Paige made her way over to Cash's table. She'd been fourteen when she'd first watched him ride a bull and sixteen before she'd gotten the nerve to talk to him. At eighteen, she'd taken him to her bed. Seven years had passed since that night. Looking at him tonight, those must have been seven long and hard years.

He looked tired and damaged. And hell, maybe more than a little dangerous to her heart. His face was grooved with wrinkles, far too many for a man of twenty-nine.

She rolled her fingers into her palm to keep from brushing his blond hair off his forehead. He needed a haircut, but then he probably needed a lot of things she couldn't provide.

"Ready to get our guest in bed?" Donald said as he reentered the bar.

When she nodded, he locked the front door and headed to the booth.

"What do I need to do?" she asked.

"Get his hat. I've got him." He grabbed Cash's arm and threw him over his shoulder in a fireman's carry. "And get the door."

Paige retrieved Cash's Stetson and hurried to the back exit. She followed the huge man through the door and locked it behind them. Donald climbed the back steps to a small efficiency apartment. He dropped Cash on the twin bed.

"That it? If so, I'm heading home."

"Thanks, Donald. Goodnight."

He closed the door as he exited, leaving her and her emotions in turmoil.

She glanced down. Strands of wavy hair flopped over Cash's brow. With no one to remind her she was supposed to hate him, she brushed them back, studying the man she'd known so long ago.

In his alcohol-induced sleep, the creases in his brow didn't seem so deep now. The etched furrows on either side of his lips eased into soft lines. But the dark circles under his eyes remained. Black and foreboding.

She pulled his dirty boots off and set them on the floor. She unbuckled the massive silver belt buckle and left his belt hanging free.

"You're a son of a bitch, Cash Montgomery," she whispered. "You destroyed my dreams the way Bad Bob destroyed yours. But seeing you like this kills me. I hope you can find the way back so I can kick your ass without feeling guilty."

Then she leaned over and kissed his lips.

THE WOMAN'S LIPS WRAPPED SNUGLY AROUND HIS rock-hard cock. He groaned and ground his head into his pillow. Her long auburn hair tickled where it flared over his thighs. He jerked his hips up and…

A sudden blast of cold water hit him in the face.

He jackknifed to sitting, sputtering and spitting water. His heart rate jacked up into a full-out gallop.

"What the fuck?" he yelled.

His brothers, Travis and Jason Montgomery, and his brother-in-law and business partner, Mitch Landry, stood at the foot of his bed. He glanced around an unfamiliar room.

"Where the fuck am I?" He shook the cold water from his dripping hair. "Where's the woman?" His eyes squinted in a harsh glare. "And why the fuck are you here?"

Travis, the oldest, lifted an eyebrow. "Not sure if the order will match the questions but you're in Leo's drunk room. Don't know nothin' about a woman. And we're here to drag your ass home."

Cash shoved the wet hair off his face. "There was a woman. I remember her. Tall. Built like a brick outhouse. Red hair."

The three men exchanged glances before Jason said, "No woman, man. Just you with your hand wrapped around your cock."

"Fuck you," Cash snarled. "Get the—"

He never finished. The sour taste of bile rose in the back of his throat. He swallowed, which did nothing for the nausea now sweeping through him. He slammed his hand over his mouth.

"Bathroom," he said through his fingers.

Travis pointed to the left over Cash's shoulder. Staggering from the bed, he just made it to the toilet before leaving the entire contents of his stomach in the bowl. He slid to the cold tile floor and rested his face on the chilly porcelain edge of the tub. His oldest brother's dusty boots came into view.

"Get out," Cash groaned. "Leave me alone."

Travis leaned over, extending a hand. "Let me help you. I've been here."

Cash slapped the hand away. "Get out," he shouted and then winced at the pain his voice inflicted on his brain.

"Fine, we'll go, but it's been six months, Cash. It's time."

Cash threw a pointed glare in Travis's direction.

"We're leaving, but you need to get up and go home. Leo wants his drunk room back."

"What time is it?" Cash choked out.

Travis turned back to him. "After noon."

"Bar's open?"

"Not for you," Travis said.

"The parents are expecting you at home today," Jason said from behind Travis. "I don't know that I'd want you in my house. You've drunk yourself from Nevada to Texas. You smell like an outhouse and look even worse."

"And fuck you too," Cash replied.

"Enough, Jason," Travis said, pushing his brother back into the small apartment. He squatted next to Cash. "I'm here when you need me. Just call."

"Unless you give a better blow job than that redhead, I won't be needin' nothin' from you."

"See you soon," Travis said with a smile, which just pissed Cash off even more.

"No, you won't," he shouted at the three men's backs as they walked away.

As soon as the door closed, Cash slid the rest of the way to the floor and curled into a ball. He didn't need his brothers or anybody. He was just fine.

Chapter Two

Paige stretched her arms over her head and then snuggled back into the thousand-thread-count sheets. Leaving this plush mattress behind when she moved out of Uncle James's house was going to be hard. As soon as her budget could swing it, buying a gel-foam mattress would shoot to the top of her must-have list.

Rolling onto her side, she slid her hand under her face and thought about seeing Cash Montgomery in Leo's last night. Would he remember her? Recognize her? It'd been a long time and she'd changed a lot from her teen years.

Seeing him in his boozed-out condition last night was the last thing she'd ever expected. He'd been king of his world. To see how far he'd let himself fall had almost made her physically ill.

She had a lot to get done today and solving the mess Cash had made out of his life wasn't on her must-do list. She swung her legs off the comfortable mattress and climbed out of bed.

After stripping and replacing the sheets on the massive king-sized bed, she finished packing the rest of her belongings, not that she had that much to pack. Living on the road with her parents in an RV for all of her life while traveling from town to town on the professional rodeo circuit had taught her exactly what was necessary versus what was a luxury.

She loaded the final few boxes, put her new kitten in the pet carrier and headed over to Angus Fitzgerald's house to see exactly what needed to be done to make it livable. Caroline Graham had warned her that no one had lived there since her great-uncle had died so the place would need a good cleaning.

The front door key was exactly where Caroline had said it would be, over the top of the door frame. Paige let herself in and looked around.

"Well, Ruby, we have a job ahead of us." She lowered her pet to the dusty hardwood floor. "Your assignment is mouse patrol," she said to her almost-six-month-old kitten. "Kill, but do not eat."

Ruby answered with a *mrrreeow* and headed toward the back of the house to explore.

Paige propped her hands on her hips and sneezed before letting out a long sigh. Where to begin? Dust covered every square inch of every exposed surface. Maybe Ruby had the right idea. Exploration first.

The front door admitted visitors into a well-used living room with a leather sofa, a couple of recliners, a scattering of tables and a fireplace that looked as though it'd hosted many fires over the years. To the right was an open door that led to a well-used office and library.

She walked farther into the living room and took a hall off to her right, which led to a small, antiquated bathroom and large bedroom. The bedroom contained a double bed, bedside tables and a dresser. All of the furniture looked antique and she suspected they'd been quality pieces when they were purchased. A dining room, old kitchen with washer and dryer and a small bedroom and bathroom with a sink and old toilet made up the remainder of the first floor. The upstairs had three unfurnished bedrooms, a sitting area and one very out-of-date bathroom.

After her quick tour, she collected Ruby and headed back to her car. This job required a powerful vacuum, which she hadn't found during her house tour, and cleaning supplies that could cut through months of built-up grime.

Two hours later, and hundreds of dollars poorer, Paige and Ruby tackled their individual assignments. Paige had her questions about Ruby's work ethics as her cat perched upon the sofa and seemed content to watch Paige clean.

Firing up the vacuum first, Paige figured she would suck up as much dirt and dust as possible before she tackled the tables, floors and walls with cleaning cloths. For the next six hours, she vacuumed, swept, washed and polished. She loaded sheets and towels into and out of the washer and dryer. Warm sheets from the dryer went directly onto the bed in the front bedroom while freshly laundered towels found new homes in the linen closet and towel racks in the bath.

At about seven p.m., she collapsed on the sofa with a loud exhale. She had put a dent into the necessary work required to get the house back into a livable condition. Many more hours of housework were needed, but today had been a step in the right direction. Independence. Reliance on herself. The start of a new job.

"Not perfect and not finished, but a good start, don't you think, Ruby?"

Ruby lifted her rear leg and began grooming.

"Thanks for your support."

A buzzing from her purse drew her attention and she leaned over the sofa arm to pull her phone out. Four missed calls. Three from her brother and one from Caroline Graham. She listened to the message from Dr. Graham, who just wanted to make sure Paige had gotten in without a problem. Her brother wanted her to call as soon as she got the message. She did.

The phone rang three times before a female said, "Leo's."

Thunderous country music blasted Paige's eardrums. "This is Paige Ryan. Who is this?"

"It's Mae. Leo's got his hands full. Said if this was you, for you to hold on for him."

"Thanks, Mae."

Paige heard a loud clunk when Mae set the phone receiver on the counter. While she waited for Leo, rowdy laughter and singing resounded through to her end. Sounded like a Thursday night crowd ready to get their weekends started. In a minute, the clatter of someone picking up the phone dimmed the noise.

"Paige?"

"Yeah. It's me. What do you need, Leo?"

"Help. The place is packed. Can you lend a hand for a few hours? One of my waitresses called in sick." When she hesitated, he added, "You don't have to close. Just come and help at the bar."

Her leg and back muscles knotted up at the thought of standing for three or four hours, but Leo had always been there for her, even when he didn't know it.

On the worst day of her life, the day they'd buried their parents, Leo had been the one who'd held her, cried with her and made her feel not so alone in the world.

On the second worst day of her life, he'd been the one to suggest she leave the rodeo road and go to college. He had no idea that he'd probably saved her sanity.

"Give me an hour and I'll come."

"Thanks, sis." He hung up before she could say anything.

Slowly, Cash opened his eyes. A Mack truck revved its engine in his head. He smacked his lips. Tasted like someone had put dog crap in his mouth while he slept…not that he really knew what that tasted like. When he tried to sit up, he found himself wedged between the toilet and bathtub. Wiggling moved his body enough to sit up, but both actions made the grinding noise in his head increase tenfold.

He dropped his head into his hands. His rancid breath collected in his lap and made him wince at the foul odor. Truly disgusting. Using the tub for leverage, he pushed himself to standing, weaving a little in the process. His damaged leg muscles spasmed and threatened to drop him back on his ass. After standing for a couple of minutes, he could put one foot in front of the other.

The progress back to the tiny bed was slow and painful, each step jarring both muscles and brain. How long had he been asleep? A quick glance out a small window showed the sun low in the sky with only its upper quadrant showing. What time was it? Five? Six? Seven? It could later for all he knew. The sun didn't set in Texas in April until after eight.

He lowered himself to the edge of the bed, supporting his head in the palms of his hands. Hell. It didn't matter what time it was. His life was over.

At twenty-nine.

Totally over.

It wasn't fair. Anger flared inside. His life sucked. He could only hope he'd die young and get it over with.

His gaze ran over his boots. Who had removed them? He sure hadn't. Squeezing his eyes together to help him think—and block any amount of light from his aching eyeballs—he would swear there'd been a woman. Very pretty. Tall. There was something about her that seemed familiar. What was it? He pushed his brain for more information but he might as well have been trying to save water in a sieve.

After shoving his feet into his boots, he headed to the bar to retrieve his keys.

Driving to a house he hadn't considered home since he'd been eighteen confirmed his total failure at life. What man his age still lived in his old bedroom in his parents' house?

Damn it. He didn't have anywhere else to go. He'd sold the motorhome he'd used to travel from rodeo to rodeo, not that it'd been much to brag about. Fifteen years old, rust encrusted and belching smoke, but it'd been his. It'd held everything he'd needed so he'd never bothered with a house or condo. He hadn't needed nor wanted the hassle of permanent roots. Big mistake. Now he had nothing and no place to call his own.

Until this very minute, it'd never bothered him that much. He'd figured he always had time set up housekeeping, once he decided where he wanted to live and with whom.

Now he wished he'd invested in a small condo. At least he could go to a place he called his own rather than to the bedroom of his childhood.

He pounded the steering wheel with his fist. What a loser. Wouldn't the other guys riding the circuit give him hell for going home to Mommy and Daddy?

To delay facing the reality of just how crappy his life had turned out, he took the long way to Bar M Ranch, circling by the Kickin' Bull Ranch, home to his sister, Olivia, her two children and her husband,

Mitch Landry. Hell, he hadn't even seen his new niece. What was she? A month old? Six weeks?

A loser, a bad uncle and a useless brother.

He turned into the Kickin' Bull Ranch drive and stopped. A female Brahma cow munched the new grass as her bull baby eyed him. He'd have sworn the little bastard sneered at him. When momma raised her head and eyeballed him too, a cold sweat broke out on his neck and trickled down his back. He tightened his fingers on the truck's steering wheel until his arms shook as if he were sitting on the San Andreas Fault during a level nine earthquake.

The Brahma momma tossed her head and let out a loud, deep bellow. Cash's heart jumped. His cold sweat became a cold flood as he shivered at the sound.

When he was capable of wrestling control of his body back from the anxiety racing through him, he slammed the truck in reverse and whipped back on the road, flying past the bellowing cow and her satanic bull baby. He didn't slow down until he reached the turn in for Bar M, his parents' ranch. He slowed, even turned on the left signal light, but it was as if the wheel was locked. It simply wouldn't turn into their drive. Then, as if possessed by independent thought, his right foot pressed hard on the accelerator and he roared past. He whipped onto the cut-off that would turn him around and head him back to Leo's bar.

One drink, he told himself. *Just one before I have to see the disappointment on my parents' faces.*

He wheeled into Leo's lot and had to circle a number of times before he could find a place to park.

Weekends around here started on Thursday night, not that the Thursday partiers didn't have to work on Friday. They did. They simply wanted to get a jump on the weekend fun.

Same as him. He was just getting a jump on the weekend.

The music from the live band was ear-splitting, the sound blasting out the door the minute Cash swung it open. The dance floor was packed with couples gyrating and one-stepping to the music. He pushed his way through until he could see the back booth. Open. He tried to look nonchalant as he hurried to claim it.

"What'll it be, sugar?" a dark-haired waitress he didn't know asked.

"Whiskey. Jack Daniels. Bring the bottle."

"Sure thang, sugar." She twisted and wiggled her hips as she walked away.

As he sank into the cushions, memories of other nights and other bars and beautiful women cluttered his mind like paper thrown into the air. One memory landing on top on another. Each one different but similar.

At one time, he'd been the draw in any bar he entered, unable to sit alone for longer than five minutes before women slid in the booth beside him, or men began shaking his hand, buying him all the drinks he could handle. The men wanted to be him and the women wanted to fuck him.

He had been a somebody.

That'd been then. Now, he was a nobody.

Worse than a nobody, actually. The men felt sorry

for him and the women wanted to mother him. Screw that.

"Here ya go," the waitress said, setting an unopened bottle of Jack Daniels and a glass on the table. "Leo started you a tab and said to get your keys."

"Fine." He fished his keys from his jeans pocket before he cracked the top. "Wait a minute," he said as she turned to leave. "Last night, there was a woman here. I'm trying to find her."

She laughed. "Honey, there are women here every night. What'd she look like?"

A heat flushed his cheeks. "I don't know. She was here alone, I know that. I need to talk to her."

"That's a tough description to match. I wasn't here last night." She tilted her head toward the other side of the room. "Sally was though. I'll ask her."

"Thanks." He poured the highball glass to the rim, drained it in one gulp and refilled it.

He'd made his way through about one-half of the bottle when Sally strode over. "Mae tells me you're looking for someone from last night?"

"Yeah. Single. I mean, she wasn't here with anyone."

Sally shook her head. "Sorry. There weren't any single women here last night. Just couples. You were pretty out of it. Maybe you just thought you met someone here."

"Never mind," he growled. "Forget it."

"Sorry I couldn't help," she said with a smile and left.

Just as well, he thought as he finished off another shot. What woman would want a broken-down has-been cowboy with a limp and no future?

He poured another drink and rested his head against the back of the booth. His life wasn't supposed to be like this. He'd had a master plan, a damn good one. Win the national bull riding championship for the third time, get a gig doing on-air commentary, maybe pick up a few endorsement contracts. He shouldn't be a washed-up ex-bull rider before he was thirty. He should be at the top of his game, master of his world. Instead, he was master of nothing.

Except, damned if he didn't own half of the cattle being raised at Kickin' Bull Ranch. The plan had been to become a stock contractor for the Professional Bull Riding association. What the hell had he been thinking going into business with Mitch Landry to raise bulls?

God, he'd come to hate the smell of cattle, the sound of cattle…hell, everything about cattle except how they tasted. If he never had to be around cattle again, he'd be a happy man.

"Hello, little brother."

Cash's head snapped so quickly he banged into the booth wall. Travis stood there looking down at him, total disgust in reflected in his expression. Cash wasn't surprised. Oh, he was surprised to see Travis in the bar, just not surprised to see the repugnance in Travis's icy stare. Even his own brother recognized Cash as the failure he was.

Cash's upper lip curled into a snarl. "What are you

doing here?" He snapped his fingers. "Let me guess. Someone called you."

Travis shrugged. "I think I might have used up all the allotted Montgomery drunk time when Susan died."

Susan, Travis's first wife, had died when she and Travis had been twenty-six. He'd spent the next year so deep in a drunken haze the family had feared they would lose him. But somehow, he made it back out and had been sober for almost ten years. Now married to Dr. Caroline Graham, they were expecting their first child soon.

"Shouldn't you be home with your pregnant wife?"

Travis slid into the booth across from Cash. His expression changed as he watched Cash drink. Was that pity in his brother's face? Shit. That'd be worse than revulsion. He'd rather be hated than pitied. "She's fine. She's worried about you, however."

"I'm fine. Tell her not to worry. Now you can go home."

Travis crossed his arms on the table. "Drinking isn't going to help."

"You're just jealous because I can control my drinking while you never could."

Cash made a show of downing a full glass of whiskey. When Travis smiled, fresh raw annoyance chewed at Cash's patience.

"Just get out, Travis. It's my life."

"Nope. I'll just sit here and wait until you pass out so I can drive you home."

"You're a bastard."

Travis leaned back and stretched his arm along the back of the booth's cushion. "I'm a drunk, Cash. I know what it is to want to drink more than to live. And I'm your brother. I'll always be here for you."

Cash glared at him. "You're going to sit there and suck all the fun out of this, aren't you?"

His brother lifted an eyebrow. "You didn't look like you were having much fun…not this morning and not when I walked in tonight."

"Fine. Let me pay my bill and get my keys."

"Bill's paid and I have your keys in my pocket."

"Well, doesn't big brother think of everything," Cash said with a sneer. "Walk slow. You know I'm a crip."

"Enough, Cash." Travis glared across at him. "You're not a cripple. Your life's not over. So your career plans have taken a turn. So what? You make the turn and see what's there. Life isn't over just because one thing didn't work out for you."

Cash twisted the glass of whiskey around in circles. "You don't understand."

"I don't understand? Bullshit." Travis pointed toward his own chest with his thumb. "You think my life plan didn't go down the toilet with Susan's death? Hell, man, life is about all the curves."

"I had a plan. It was a great plan." He downed the booze in one swallow. "Now I don't have shit. No life. A gimp leg. Hell, I don't even have a house to call my own." He refilled his glass and poured a little pity along with the liquor down his throat.

Travis leaned across the table. "Tell you what. Go see the parents tonight. If that's intolerable for you, I know of somewhere else to crash for a while."

"Fine."

"C'mon. Let's get going."

The men stood, Cash weaving a little on his feet. "Still wish I could find that woman from last night," he said.

Travis laughed and slung an arm around Cash's shoulders. "Good luck, bro."

As they zigzagged around dancing bar patrons, Cash thought he got a glimpse of long auburn hair behind the bar. His heart skipped a beat at the memory. He twisted around, tried to find the woman, but in the crush of bodies, it was impossible to see his own feet, much less a woman from his past.

Hell, what would she be doing here? What were the chances? Absolutely none.

He followed Travis out to a low-slung Porsche.

"Hey," Cash said with a laugh. "How did you get this back from your wife?"

Travis grinned as the engine growled. "She's too pregnant to get in and out. Had to buy her a new SUV."

He pulled from Leo's parking lot and headed out of Whispering Springs.

"I had an idea. Can I run something past you?" Cash asked.

"Sure."

"What about the old Fitzgerald ranch?"

"What about it?"

"Can I stay there for a while?" Cash's heart clung to his ribs as he awaited his brother's response. When he'd driven by Singing Springs Ranch today and seen the old house, the idea of living there had taken root in his head. If Travis said no, he wasn't sure where he would end up.

"I don't see why not." Travis glanced at Cash. "You realize the place has been empty for almost a year, right? Probably dust and dirt an inch thick."

"But it's got furniture, right? And electricity and water?"

"Yes. It's pretty much as Angus left it when he died."

"And your wife won't mind?"

Travis's wife, Caroline, had inherited Singing Springs Ranch when her great-uncle Angus Fitzgerald had died.

"Doubt it. She's got a soft spot in her heart for the old place. She'll be glad to have someone in there. I'll—"

Whatever Travis was going to say was cut off by the ringing of his cell phone. He fished his cell from his front jeans pocket and checked the caller ID.

"Hey, babe. I'm on my way. Need anything?"

Cash could hear his sister-in-law's voice coming from Travis's phone but couldn't understand what she was saying. But he noticed the rising tension in Travis's voice.

"When? Okay. Okay. I'm on my way. Hang on." He slammed the accelerator to the floor. The sudden speed pressed Cash firmly into his seat back.

"What happened?"

"Caroline's in labor. Her water broke."

"Crap. Is that bad?"

Travis laughed. "I have no idea." He took a corner sharply, throwing Cash into the passenger door. "But I don't think so."

Cash grinned. "Can't believe you're going to be a father."

Travis let out a loud whoop. "Me neither."

They made it to Halo M Ranch in record time, flying down the drive to come to an abrupt stop in front of the house. Caroline's SUV was parked in front, her hospital bag on the porch. Travis slammed the car into park and jumped from the car like it was on fire.

"Caroline," he shouted.

A very pregnant Caroline Graham waddled out the door. "Calm down, honey. We have plenty of time."

Travis cleared the front steps in a hurdle. "Got everything?" he asked as he helped his wife down the stairs.

She smiled and patted his cheek. "I've got you. That's all I need right now."

Cash's heart seized at the scene unfolding in front of him. His older, tougher, always-calm brother was totally losing his cool. He smiled. He'd never seen Travis so excited and scared at the same time. The only thing Cash could equate the feeling to was climbing on the back of a bull…adrenaline-driven fear. And damn if he didn't miss it sometimes.

"What can I do to help?" he asked. Cash was totally out of his league.

"Hi, Cash," Caroline said and headed in his direction.

"Where are you going?" Travis asked, his voice laced with anxiety. "We can't take the Porsche."

Caroline smiled and patted his arm. "I just wanted to give my brother-in-law a hug."

"Make it snappy," Travis growled. "I do not want to have these babies here."

Caroline laughed and then hugged Cash. "So good to see you. I've been worried about you. You okay?"

"Yes, ma'am," Cash lied. "I'm doing just great."

"Now can we go?" Travis snapped.

Caroline shook her head. "First-time deliveries take forever, Travis." She turned to walk to her SUV then turned back to Cash. "Can you do me a favor?"

"Anything."

"My brother. Can you get him to the hospital later?"

"Sure. No problem."

"You might want to call Mom," Travis said. "I'd tell you to call Olivia and Jason, but I suspect Mom's dialing finger is much faster than yours."

Cash chuckled. "Glad to help."

A teenage boy with long brown hair stood on the porch watching all the activity in the drive. As soon as Travis and Caroline left, Cash walked up onto the porch.

"You must be Caroline's brother," he said with a grin. "Noah, if I remember correctly."

The boy nodded. "Yep. And you're Cash, the little brother."

"Well, now that we both know who we are, we'd better get to those phone calls." Cash moved toward the door and then noticed Noah hadn't moved. "Problem?"

"No. Yes."

Cash looked at the teen's ashen face. "Worried about your sister?"

Noah let out a long breath of air. "Yes. What if something happens?"

Cash knew a little about Caroline and Noah's history…that their parents lived in a third-world country on a missionary trip and that Caroline and Noah had been raised by their maternal grandmother who'd died last year.

He slung his arm around Noah. "She'll be fine. And hey, we're both going to be uncles."

Noah looked at him, his nostrils flaring. "Are you drunk? You smell like it."

"I've had a drink or two," Cash lied. "No biggie."

"Well, I'm going to the hospital and one of us has to drive." He shook off Cash's arm. "And I'm not riding with a drunk driver. I'll take my chances driving myself."

"No way, pal. I can drive. Let's go make those phone calls."

By the time Cash had poured a couple of cups of coffee down his throat and called his parents and siblings, it was close to ten p.m. The effects of the alcohol were waning, but he decided Travis's truck might be the safest vehicle to borrow should he bump the fender or something.

When Noah flashed his restricted driver's license, which gave him the right to drive with a licensed adult driver in the car, Cash handed over the keys with unexpressed relief. When they got to the hospital maternity waiting room, his entire family had already beaten them there.

He hugged his sister. "Who's got the kids?"

"Magda. And I'm more than a little pissed at you. You haven't even been by to see Eliza Grace."

Cash felt the flush as it climbed up his neck. He hung his head. "Yeah. Sorry."

"Cash." His mother hugged him. "I'm glad you're here."

"Have you heard anything?"

"Hi, Noah," Jackie Montgomery said. "No, nothing yet. Travis came out a couple of minutes ago to say everything was going fine." She put her arm around the teen. "Come sit with me. I'm a nervous wreck. You can keep me company."

Jackie hauled Noah over to some chairs where her husband sat.

"Where's Lydia?" Cash asked his brother, Jason.

Dr. Lydia Henson was Caroline Graham's medical-practice partner and his brother's long-term fiancée.

Jason pointed with his chin toward a couple of

doors. "In the back. We just got here and she wanted to check in with Olivia."

The Montgomery clan filled most of the chairs in the small waiting room, individual conversations floating around the room. Cash observed his family. He'd been on the rodeo road for years. Even his teenage years had been one junior rodeo after another. He'd loved his life, even though he now realized how much he'd missed.

He'd made Olivia and Mitch's wedding but only for the day, having to fly back to catch up with the PBR circuit. As his sister had pointed out, he hadn't met his new niece yet, and Adam, Olivia and Mitch's son, changed every time he saw the kid.

The alcohol buzz was gone, leaving a pounding headache in its place. Resting his head on the wall, Cash shut his eyes and remembered the only girl who'd looked at him the way Caroline looked at Travis, or Mitch looked at Olivia. All that love displayed for the world to see.

But she'd been too young. Hell, he'd been too young and too full of himself to admit how deeply she'd crawled into his soul. One night together and he'd run.

No, what he'd done had been much worse than that. He squeezed his eyes tight as if that could dim the memory, but nothing could blunt the shame he still felt.

The reality was he hadn't run. Instead, he had treated her like every other buckle bunny on the circuit with flippant comments and a pat on the ass the next morning. He'd made sure never to find himself alone with her, always using one woman or another to serve as a buffer. He'd been overwhelmed by his feelings. He couldn't face her or his damn reactions to that night together.

But she'd been far from a woman who considered fucking a cowboy another notch on her belt. She'd been a beautiful young woman just reaching her maturity.

Paige Ryan. The rodeo vet's daughter. He'd watched Paige grow from gangly teen to a mature, stunning woman. Tall. Auburn hair. Piercing green eyes. A mouth made for kissing and a body made for sex.

Cash had been her first lover. He hadn't known that when they'd hit the sheets on her eighteen birthday. That'd been only the first shock of the evening.

The second shock had been the feelings she'd evoked from him. An urge to protect her from the world and its ugliness. A rightness he'd never felt with another woman. A yearning to make her his. All that had scared him shitless and he'd bolted.

His heart had skipped a beat when he'd thought he'd seen her tonight at Leo's. He scoffed. Maybe Travis was right. Maybe the whiskey had dulled his head and his vision.

The electronic swish of mechanical doors opening brought Cash back to the maternity delivery room. All gazes shot to Lydia when she walked through from the birthing suite doors.

"What's going on?" Jackie asked, springing from her chair.

Lydia smiled. "She's making progress. Probably won't be long now. She was pushing when I left."

At three a.m., Travis strode through the doors carrying two wrapped bundles.

"I would like for you all to meet Austin and Britney Montgomery."

Chapter Three

It was close to three in the morning by the time Paige finished work at Leo's bar. Every muscle in her body screamed in exhausted agony. Her eyes felt like someone had sucked out all the moisture and replaced it with sand. Her feet and hands cramped. She knew she'd be making drinks all night long in her dreams.

She let herself in and headed straight for the shower to wash away the smell of booze and sweat. It'd been a rough night, but then Thursday nights were usually cram packed with partiers and tonight had been no exception.

Giving Leo a hand when he was short-staffed or busy wasn't a problem. She'd do just about anything for her older brother. Besides, it wasn't as if her social life was booked solid. She didn't date. Didn't belong to social clubs. Wasn't part of the Whispering Springs Junior League. Wasn't involved in the women's groups at church. Crap. Now that she allowed herself to think about it, she didn't much of a life at all. How pitiful. She really needed to do something about that.

Bending at the waist, she slid her soapy cloth down her legs and for some reason the image of a couple of cowboy hats passing through the crowd flashed before her. A definite tingle hit the area between her thighs. When she'd gotten a fast glimpse of Cash walking alongside his brother, a punch to her chest had slammed the air from her lungs. Damn Cash Montgomery. She hated that he could still make her breathless with need.

She dragged the wash cloth up her leg. Part of her had been disappointed that he was on the way out. Mostly, however, she'd been glad to see him leave. If last night was any indication of how much he was drinking these days, he didn't need to be in Leo's, or any bar. He'd been a party hound back when she'd known him better. She'd hoped he'd outgrown some of that. Sadly, it seemed he'd only gotten worse.

She stepped from the shower and snagged a towel from the linen storage. Her arms were almost too tired to rub the water off. Thank goodness, she had Friday off. Her to-do list was almost as long as her arm.

After putting on her favorite sleep shirt, she headed for her bed. Of course, Ruby had beaten her there and was curled into a tight ball on one of the pillows. Paige took the other one and crashed.

Friday passed in a blur of errands. She spent the evening at Leo's Bar and Grill, another nail in her I-have-no-life coffin. When she got home at midnight, she scooted her bed-hog kitten over and climbed under the covers.

That was the last thing she knew until the Saturday morning sun burned into her eyelids. Paige moaned and rolled away from the window, trying desperately to get back into her dream involving a cowboy, some rope and a feather bed. After noticing the small movement from her owner, Ruby wrapped her tiny fur body around Paige's head and turned on the purr machine.

Paige shoved Ruby off her head with a laugh. "I'm up. I'm up," she said, swinging her bare feet to the floor. She stretched her arms toward the ceiling and looked around her room and smiled. Her own room in her own house. No sharing the hot water with anyone. No dirty dishes in the sink that didn't belong to her. No bra required if she didn't feel like putting one on. In fact, she could walk around in nothing but her extra-large T-shirt that read *Rope Me, Cowboy* and a pair of panties. No robe needed. Freedom to do whatever she wanted.

Staying at her Uncle James's house for these past ten months had been great, but she'd never forgotten she was a guest, even when she'd been there alone. But this place? This was *her* place. Caroline had told her to make herself at home, and Paige intended to do just that.

After sliding her feet into a pair of scuffs, she headed for the kitchen to start a pot of coffee. She'd make a list of things she still needed to do and supplies she needed to buy while she got her morning caffeine fix. As the coffee dripped, she turned the oven on to preheat and started bacon frying in a large skillet.

She stole the first cup of java before the pot finished filling. Her eyebrows shot up with the first sip. Stout, to say the least. She added a little water to the coffee maker's reservoir then cracked open a can of biscuits. When the preheat bell chimed, she slid a cookie sheet loaded with biscuit dough into the hot oven.

She flipped the bacon and then sat at the table with a notepad and pencil. Other than the sizzle from the bacon and the slight tick of the coffee maker, the peace was comfortable. Leaning back in the high-backed kitchen chair, she stretched out her legs and took a long sip of black coffee.

Across the table and directly in front of her, the door to the back bedroom banged open and a half-dressed man ran out, a tennis racket raised high above his head, all while he yelled, "What the hell are you doing in this house?"

Paige jumped from her chair, sending it over backwards. She spat the coffee in her mouth across the table while at the same time tossing the mug of hot liquid at her attacker. The man leapt to the side, avoiding most of the scalding java.

"What are you doing here?" she gasped out, barely able to catch her breath from the sudden adrenaline jolt, not to mention the masculine sight standing in front of her. Her heart grabbed her ribs and rattled. She struggled to focus as her mind refused to accept what she was seeing.

Cash Montgomery wore only a pair of white boxer briefs. Angry long scars crisscrossed his chest, abdomen and arms. But even those couldn't diminish the impact of his naked, chiseled six-pack. Paige swallowed hard against the rising lust.

"I live here," he answered, lowering his impromptu weapon to his side. Confusion covered his face and his brow furrowed. "Paige?
Paige Ryan?"

She nodded. "That'd be me."

His gaze roved down her body and back up to her face. "Why are you in my house? And why don't you have on clothes? Not that I'm complaining, mind you." A wolfish grin spread across his mouth. "Nice T-shirt slogan."

Paige looked down and felt the flush of embarrassment as it climbed her neck and face. Both nipples protruded through the thin material far enough to be used as hat pegs. Her gaze flew back to him. "I'll be right back."

She hurried from the kitchen, tugging down the hem of her T-shirt over her purple panties. She could barely think about the need for a robe when her mind swirled like a blender, mixing her thoughts and emotions like a smoothie.

What was Cash Montgomery doing in her house?

And more importantly, why was she kind of excited to see him? The man had practically ruined her life. Well, maybe not ruined as much as shoved her onto a new life path. Still, he'd let her fall in love with him, taken her virginity and then treated her like she had meant nothing to him. He'd broken her heart and hadn't seemed to care one whit.

Of course, she'd felt sorry for him passed out in the bar, just like she'd feel sympathy for any injured animal. And of course, she'd been crushed when she'd heard about his accident, but that didn't mean she wanted to be in close proximity to him.

Cash Montgomery was a dangerous man. Dangerous to her positive self-esteem, which she needed to prosper in the intensive graduate nursing program she'd be starting in three months. Dangerous to her plans to stay focused only on her career for now. And dangerous to her self-preservation, as her heart tended to overrule her mind when it came to Cash. Nothing good could come of him being here.

She'd thought she would be able to handle seeing him, but she'd possibly misjudged. He had to go before any decisions were made by her heart and not her head.

After grabbing her chenille robe off the bathroom door, she stood in her bedroom collecting herself before walking calmly back to the kitchen. The coffee spewed and thrown at him had been cleaned up. Her overturned chair was back upright and in its place. Cash had put on a pair of jeans and a black T-shirt that stretched to cover his broad shoulders. She'd been wrong when she'd thought he'd looked emaciated the other night. Must have been positional, because every movement had another muscle popping out somewhere new on his body.

He sat at the table, his legs stretched out in front of

him, his bare feet crossed at the ankles. He nursed a cup of black coffee like it was any morning in any town, USA. She clutched both sides of her robe, pulling them together like a virginal prude.

A battle raged in her mind.

Don't pull that robe together like you've never been with a man before. You're being ridiculous. He's seen everything you've got.

True, the opposition retorted, *but he was pretty drunk that night and seven years have passed since then. And he took your heart and stomped on it with his size-fourteen cowboy boots.*

"Are you just going to stand there and stare at me?" Cash asked with a lift of an eyebrow.

Paige whipped around to get another mug from the cabinet. After pouring her second cup of the day, she sat down.

"Let's get one thing straight," she said, sounding all the world like a school teacher reprimanding a student. "This is my house. Caroline rented it to me on Monday."

"Travis told me I could stay here for a while."

"Well, this isn't going to work at all," she said in a stiff voice that would have made a nun proud. "You'll have to make other arrangements."

He sat his cup on the table and leaned toward her. If he meant to intimidate her, it wasn't going to work. She held her position and returned his stare with one she hoped conveyed her determination to stay put in this house.

"*You'll* have to make other arrangements," he said.

"My brother owns this house and he gave it to me to live in as long as I want."

Her heart dropped into her gut. The boa-constrictor-like squeeze around her chest pulled tight. Drawing in air was an effort, as was forming coherent sentences in his presence.

"Sorry, cowboy. I'm here to stay. You're the one who has to go," she finally managed to squeak out. "You have family you could stay with until you buy yourself somewhere else to live. Use some of that butt load of money you made riding those damn bulls to get your own place instead of trying to steal mine."

"Steal? Yours?" He gave her a derisive snort. Using his cup, he pointed around the room. "This house doesn't belong to you. It's Montgomery property."

Shoving her chair back with a loud scrape on the hardwood, she stood. "I'm going to get dressed and run some errands. When I get back, I expect you to be gone. And you can rest assured that I'll be calling Caroline today." She turned and marched out of the room.

"One of your errands should be finding another place to live," he shouted at her back. "I'm not leaving. And don't call Caroline. She had twins early yesterday morning. Don't bother them today."

Paige leaned against her closed bedroom door, her hand pressed to her chest, her heart in a runaway gallop. Crap. Surely one phone call to Caroline or Travis would clear this mess up. But that wasn't going to happen. How could she dump her Cash problem on Caroline with her still in the hospital after delivery...at least she assumed Caroline was still there. Today it seemed like new mothers and babies were punted out the door fairly quickly.

Then Cash's words registered. Caroline had delivered twins.

She stepped away from the door and began sliding hangers in the closet. She was going baby-clothes shopping.

Cash hadn't said if the twins were boys or girls or one of each and she certainly couldn't go ask him. She'd just decided she wasn't speaking to him.

She pulled a tan skirt off its hanger and found a simple white blouse to go with it. Throw on a pair of sandals and some light make-up and she'd be ready to face the world...or Cash, if she had to.

Lucky for her, she didn't see her uninvited roommate when she left the house. After a stop to get flowers for the new mother and receiving blankets and sleepers—in green and yellow since she still didn't know the sex of the newborns—Paige headed for the small local hospital.

Caroline was sitting up in the bed, one baby at her breast and the other fussing in a bedside bassinet.

"Knock, knock. Am I intruding?" Paige asked from the door. "I can come back later."

Caroline looked toward her. Her smile was almost beatific. Her face radiated pure joy.

"Don't go. Come on in. Your timing is perfect. Travis left to go home and change clothes and I'm here by myself."

Paige stepped into the room carrying the two gift bags and the vase of flowers. She set the big bouquet of flowers on the window ledge with quite a few others. "Looks like my flower idea isn't that original." She held up the gift bags. "These aren't either, but you'll need lots of them," She placed the bags on the bedside table. "You can look at those later." She put her hands on her hips and grinned. "By yourself, huh? I'd say it'll be years before you'll be by yourself again."

Stroking her newborn's downy head, Caroline nodded. "And I'll love every minute of those years." She kissed the baby's head.

"Looks like you've got an unhappy one over here," Paige said walking to the squirming baby. "Hey, precious," she cooed. "What's the problem?" She stroked the baby's head. "Can I pick him up? Or is it her? I didn't even know you were having twins. You sure do know how to keep a secret."

Caroline chuckled. "Let me introduce you. In my lap is Mr. Austin Montgomery. Wiggling under your hand is Ms. Britney Montgomery. And, yes, please pick her up but you might want to check her diaper first."

"Hello, Britney," Paige said in a soothing voice. "Let's check that diaper." Finding Britney's diaper wet, Paige put on a fresh one before pressing the tiny infant against her chest. "Oh, she's so pretty," she said as she nuzzled Britney's head. "I love the smell of newborns. I think they smell like innocence."

Caroline chuckled again. "Yeah, well, if you'd

pushed these two out, you wouldn't think them so innocent."

"That's okay," she cooed to the baby tucked under her chin. "Your momma doesn't mean it." She made her way to the room's rocking chair and sat. "God, I love babies," Paige said after setting the chair moving with her foot. "Especially those I can play with and give back."

Caroline giggled. "Did you get into the house okay?"

Paige studied the glow on her friend's face and knew there was no way she was going to bring any worries into this room.

"Not a problem." *If you don't count the uninvited and unwanted and way-too-sexy roommate.*

"I bet it was filthy."

Paige shrugged. "Pretty much what you would expect for a house that's been empty for a while."

The door opened to admit a ridiculously happy Travis Montgomery. He stepped to the bed to kiss his wife before turning to Paige.

"Good morning. You're looking mighty fine this morning."

Paige laughed. "You're in a mighty fine mood this morning."

He took a sleeping Austin from his mother's arms to snuggle. "That's 'cause I've got a mighty fine wife and two—count 'em—two children." He kissed the top of Austin's head. "How's my little man?"

"Your little man can poop like one of your horses," Caroline said.

"Good boy," Travis cooed.

"And your daughter can belch like her Uncle Jason."

"Genetics comes through again."

Paige stood. "I've got to get moving. I just wanted to drop off those gifts."

"Hold on. Let me open them." Caroline dragged both gift bags into her bed. From the first, she pulled the two receiving blankets and two newborn sleepers. "Thank you," Caroline said. "I'm pretty sure we can't have too many of these."

"Check the other bag," Paige suggested.

Caroline pulled out a long, sheer, sexy black nightgown. "Oh. That's beautiful." She held the gown up to Travis. "Paige got you something too."

Travis whistled. "I'm gonna look good in that."

Caroline rolled her eyes at Paige, which made both women laugh.

"Thanks again for coming by," Caroline said. "I'm glad to hear my uncle's place is going to work for you."

"What are you talking about?" Travis said.

"I meant to tell you but it totally slipped my mind. I've rented Angus's house to Paige for a while. You know I hated letting it sit there to rot. I'm thrilled someone's making good use of it."

"But—"

Paige gave Travis a pair of wide eyes and a subtle shake of her head. "Thanks again, Caroline. I'll take good care of it." She stood. "Do you want Britney back in the bassinet or in your bed?"

Caroline held out her arms. "Here."

Paige transferred the now sleeping baby to her mother and headed for the door.

"I'll be right back," Travis said to his wife, laying a sleeping Austin in his crib. "I need to have a word with Paige."

Caroline lifted her eyebrows. "About?"

"A couple of things about Angus's house. Where the water shut-off valves are in case of an emergency, things like that."

Caroline nodded. "Good idea."

Travis followed Paige into the hall. "Listen, I don't know how to tell you this—"

"You mean that you told your brother he could live in that house also?" Paige asked.

"Yeah. That'd be it." Travis removed his hat and ran his fingers through his hair. "I had no idea that Caroline had rented it to you. I'm sorry. My little brother is going through a rough patch and—"

"I know. I've seen his rough patch, mostly passed out at Leo's."

"Look," Travis said, his eyes bright with an idea. "Let Cash stay. I'll pay you to keep an eye on him." When she arched her eyebrows in question, he continued. "No. Not like that. Just make sure he has food in the house. Somewhere to sleep. Neither of us can make him not drink, but I'd appreciate it if you didn't keep liquor in the house."

"So you're asking me to be a spy for you? Report what Cash is doing? I can't do that. Won't do that."

"No. Nothing like that. God, I don't want reports."

He chuckled. "But with you there, I won't have to worry if he's eating or dead on the floor."

When she hesitated, he added. "I know about your degrees in psychology and nursing. Caroline was impressed with your education. She told me about you while you were interviewing with the clinic. So I figure with your education, you'd understand what Cash is going through. Be able to help him deal, or at least you probably won't kill him like the rest of us want to." He touched her arm. "He's fallen into a deep hole, Paige. A really deep place. I would be there for him more if I could, but with Caroline and the new babies and all…I just need a little help. Please."

"Okay, Travis." She put her hand over his resting on his arm. "I'll figure out some way to make it work. It'll only be temporary anyway. I'm supposed to start a graduate nurse practitioner program in the fall provided I can get all my financing in order."

"I think I can help there. How does this sound? No rent since Cash isn't paying any. That's only fair. I'll pay you a thousand a month, which should cover his food, utilities and whatever. You can save the rest for your fall tuition."

"Deal."

His gaze went over her shoulder. "Speak of the devil."

Paige turned to see Cash striding toward them. So not fair that her heart rate doubled just seeing him. His limp drove an arrow into her gut.

"What are you doing here?" His lips twisted into a

snarl. “Running to tattle to Caroline? I told you to leave her alone with this.”

“My God, Cash. What the hell is wrong with you?” Travis snapped. “Paige is a good friend of my wife’s.”

Cash whipped around to face his brother. “I told her not to bother Caroline with anything right now.”

“You mean anything like your moving into Caroline’s uncle’s house?” Travis held up a hand before Cash could reply. “Paige didn’t say a word to Caroline. In fact, she didn’t say a word to me. Caroline just mentioned that she’d rented the house to Paige. My wife doesn’t know that I lent the house to you.”

Cash raked his fingers through his hair. “So what now?”

“Your brother has made me a very fair offer. We’ll share the house.”

“Share?” Cash whipped his gaze toward her.

His steamy stare was as if a hot desert wind had blown across her face. Beads of moisture popped on her brow.

“That’s right,” Travis said. “Share. Paige will pay the same rent you are paying, which happens to be nothing.”

“It’s not going to be forever.” Paige fought the rise of panic churning in her gut. Tightening a hold on her emotions, she continued. “I’ll be going back to school in the fall, so we’re talking only four months or so.” Her mouth tugged into a forced smile. “I’m sure we can keep from strangling each other until then.”

Cash narrowed his eyes slightly but the fire there

was barely banked. "Fine. We'll make it work." His gaze dropped to his boots before lifting to meet Paige's eyes. "I apologize. I seem to lose my temper more than I used to."

Paige held out her hand, grateful to see no shaking in her arm. "Accepted."

Their hands touched. A zing of newly awakened arousal zapped her. The jolt of energy struck her heart. For a second it quivered, and then its rate took off like a racehorse out of the chute.

Paige gave his rough hand a quick shake and dropped it. "I've got to run. Errands to do. People to see." She looked at Travis. "We will be fine. I've had roommates before. I know how to whip them into shape."

Cash grinned and Paige wanted to groan with longing for the man. She left before her lust put words in her mouth.

Both men watched Paige walk to the elevator.

"She has a nice walk," Travis observed.

Cash slapped his shoulder. "Hey. You're a new father. You don't get to notice things like that."

Travis threw his arm around his little brother. "I'll notice things like that until they close the lid on my casket. Now, want to see my kids?"

"Naw," Cash said. "I came to see your wife."

A COUPLE OF HOURS LATER, CASH WALKED INTO A quiet house. "Paige? You here?"

No answer, except for a meow.

"Damn. She has a cat," he muttered as he hung his jacket on the post of the stair railing.

Paige Ryan. What a cruel bitch fate was. He'd pretty much counted on never seeing her again. But now? Damned if he wouldn't see her every day.

At least for the moment, he had the house to himself. It'd been years since he'd been in the old Fitzgerald's house. *Before* his roommate got back might be the best time for a little exploring.

He remembered the layout from the very few times he'd been here as a child. He walked through the downstairs area and, other than the room he'd slept in, all the rooms were clean, dust-free and fresh-smelling. With every step, the small grey kitten ran ahead of him and waited to grab the leg of his jeans.

When he found Paige's room, he allowed himself a minute to breathe in the scent. A little floral perfume. A whole lot of Paige. He leaned against the doorjamb and studied the old-fashioned chenille bedspread covering her made bed. The kitten jumped on it and curled into the pillows.

Cash sighed. Seemed like he'd known Paige forever. Had watched her grow up. She'd just turned fourteen when he'd joined the pro rodeo circuit and what a beauty she'd been then. Time had only served to mold her figure into curves and dips men loved.

She'd had a crush on him back when she was sixteen. He'd given her a very chaste happy-birthday kiss and her embarrassed flush had been cute to watch. But he'd enjoyed the feel of his lips on hers too much. She'd been only a teenager. By then, he was a twenty-year-old with too many notches on his bedpost.

He probably shouldn't have done it. Nonetheless, he couldn't stop himself from opening her closet door. There, hanging from a nail driven into the door's wood, was a belt…and a silver rodeo buckle. His belt. His buckle. She'd kept it even after he'd walked out on her.

A soul-searing bomb detonated in his gut. The breath rushed from his lungs and the band around his chest made it impossible to draw in another.

He stumbled back and turned away from his find. He didn't want to remember her eighteenth birthday. Didn't want to remember what a jackass he'd been. Didn't want to see the pain in her eyes that night. Didn't want the memory of her expression every time their paths crossed for the next couple of weeks.

Walking back to the living room, he looked at the stairs. Yes, with the damage to his leg, they would be a bitch to climb every day. On the other hand, the doctor had advised him to get back to normal. Plus, even though they'd be sharing space, he'd be on a different level.

He climbed the stairs, his left leg muscles whimpering. He wanted a drink. One beer. One whiskey. Something that'd take his mind off the pain.

Instead, he continued to climb until he reached the second level of the house. Three bedrooms, one bath. No furniture. One open area that overlooked the living room.

He opened a door in the overlook area and found

another set of steps. As he climbed these, the years of accumulated dust brought tears and sneezes. Something tickled his cheek. He swiped at it and found a long string that turned on the sole light.

When his eyes cleared of tears, he walked around in the attic. Freshly stirred-up dust was his major accomplishment. All that was stored in this area were broken lamps, a couple of large sea chests and an old table set that needed to be totally rebuilt. No extra bedroom furniture or anything he could use in the upstairs sitting area. He shrugged. Just as well. The bed in that back bedroom had been pretty damn lumpy and uncomfortable. He'd slept in horrible places over his years of travel. He'd have to add his current bed to the list.

After another round of sneezing, he sat at the opening of the stairs to mentally compile a list of what he needed to buy to renovate the upstairs.

"Cash?" You here?" Paige's soft, Southern drawl floated upstairs and infiltrated his gut. He'd had to remember to keep his distance. She was on an escalator up in her life while he was in total freefall. No sense to pull her down with him.

"Up here."

"Where?" Her footfalls tapped on each wooden step as she made her way up.

"The attic."

Her heart-shaped face appeared at the base of the stairs. "I haven't been up there yet."

"You're not missing anything." He sneezed. "Lots

of dust and a few pieces of broken furniture." He stood. "I'll come down."

She hurried up the staircase. "No. Stay. I want to see."

He retook his seat and scooted to the left. His eyes were at the perfect level to admire her trim, shapely legs as she stepped past him. He fought the urge to stroke her calf. He bet it'd be soft and smooth like the finest silk. He thought about running his tongue from her ankle up to the junction where her thigh met her hip; Imagined how sweet her flesh would taste. How sensitive she'd be to his touch.

She sneezed, breaking him out of his daydream and none too soon as he'd begun to get hard at the thought of her. He wasn't doing so good with the keep-his-distance plan.

"You weren't kidding," she said after a second sneeze. She turned in a full circle, taking in the view. "I wonder if the Fitzgeralds had set this area aside in case the two bedrooms below weren't enough."

He shrugged. "No clue. They never had any kids."

Nodding, she said, "I know. It's kind of sad when you think about it."

"I suppose."

She sat down at the stair opening, dropping her legs down until her feet rested on the second step. "We need to talk."

If there was ever a sentence that could strike panic in the soul of every man, it'd be that one.

Chapter Four

Cash had no reason to panic in response to her request to talk, so why did his gut screw tight and his lungs fail to fully inflate? He wasn't leaving here until he was good and ready. He braced himself for battle.

"Yeah? About what?" The edge in his voice was sharp enough to slice paper.

She tilted her head to one side and smiled, but her smile held a tinge of sadness. "Your leg."

"My leg is just fine," he snapped, irritation burning his gut and effectively dousing any manners he might have. Flashing an angry glare, he added, "I don't want to talk about it either."

She laid her hand on the knee of his injured leg, her heat searing through his jeans like a hot iron. "Let me say what I want to say and it'll be done. I watched your last ride on television. It's a miracle you're alive. An honest-to-God miracle."

He turned his face away, refusing to look her in the eye. Reliving that night was like volunteering to sweep the floors of hell. No man in his right mind would want to remember the night his life had ceased to have meaning. Wasn't it bad enough that his dreams replayed the accident over and over? Did he have to talk about it while he was awake too?

She pulled her hand away but continued, uncaring or unknowing what this conversation was costing him.

"When you went into the well, I figured the ride was over. Then the people in the stands closest to the well gasped and that's when I knew you hadn't fallen off Bad Bob but were trapped."

"Stop. That's enough," he growled. It'd all happened so fast. The left spin instead of the bull's usual right spin. The unexpected buck. The sensation of flying through the air. The abrupt stop when he crashed into the gate. The grit of dirt in his mouth. The shock of pain as Bad Bob lived up to his name, stomping on Cash over and over. As the memories flooded back, his heart raced with fear and anxiety. His breathing hitched. He shut his eyes and drew in a deep breath.

"That's enough," he repeated softer than before. "I remember. I was there."

But she wouldn't stop. "I watched you get hurt. The announcers played it over and over and then again in slow motion." A catch in her voice made him turn back to her. Cash could see the tears glistening in her eyes. "I thought you were dead. That I'd never see you again. I wanted to kill that sonofabitch bull."

He couldn't help it. He smiled. "Bad Boy was just doing his job. I'm the one who fucked up. Not him." *And I'm still fucked up.* But he didn't say that aloud. Didn't need to. Everybody who got close to him could see he was damaged beyond repair.

"I kept meaning to send you a note while you were in the hospital but—" she shrugged, "—I didn't know what to say. I kept putting it off and putting it off until it seemed pointless to say anything. I feel bad about that."

He rocked his knee over until it tapped hers. "Don't worry about it. That's in the past. But…" He drew in a breath before he continued, "as long as we're on the subject of history and things we regret…"

She looked at him but didn't say anything.

"I should have called you after your parents' accident. I should have told you how sorry I was when I heard."

Her face froze into a sad mask.

"I…I loved your parents. They were special people. As soon as I heard about their deaths, I should have reached out to you. I just didn't know what to say either. I was too far away to make the funeral. We, you and I, hadn't spoken in years. I wasn't sure if you'd even want to hear from me."

"That's okay. I understand," she said, her voice thin.

"No, it's not okay." He mimicked her action and laid a hand on her knee. As soft as he'd imagined her skin might be, it was softer, silkier. The floral bouquet of her skin lotion drifted to his nostrils. He inhaled, filled his lungs with her scent.

Her gaze dropped to his hand. For a moment, her breath held and then she sucked in a deep intake of air. Under his hand, her flesh rose in goose bumps and her leg gave a slight shake.

Was she affected by his touch? Or, God forbid, was she repulsed by it? By him? By his damn limp?

Did she think that his life was over too? Or worse, did she feel pity for him?

He'd rather she be repulsed by what an asshole he'd been in the past than pity the man he was today.

He removed his hand. "Anyway, I just wanted to say how sorry I was when I heard and to tell you how special they were. Not just to me, but to all of us riding the circuit."

"Thanks," she said, standing. She looked down at him. "Well, on to how to make this work. I think I should move upstairs. It'd be better for your…well, I mean—"

Damn it. Pity etched her expression. She did feel sorry for him and that just made him more determined to not live downstairs.

"I'm taking the upstairs," he said, interrupting her. He held up a hand when she opened her mouth. "No. I want it. Besides, it'll be good for my leg to get the exercise of going up and down stairs."

"Well, that's true, I guess." She sneezed. "Let's go down and see what needs to be done to make it habitable." She took one step down, sneezed and then wiped her nose. "Now you see why the downstairs got cleaned before I stayed here. Dust makes me sneeze."

He chuckled, determined to make her see him as something more than a damaged cowboy. "Then I'd suggest you never come upstairs once I get settled in. I'm not the world's best housekeeper."

They walked through the attic door into the area overlooking the living room. Footprints, his and hers, tracked in the floor dust. Numerous small kitten prints wound through each room.

He pointed at them. "The cat's been exploring too."

"Ruby. Her name is Ruby."

He nodded as he continued to study the different foot patterns. From the direction of Paige's prints, he could tell she'd come directly to him in the attic. For some reason, that she hadn't looked in all the rooms seemed significant…as though finding him had been important to her.

"So, what's your plan?" she asked looking around at the closed doors. "Looks like you went into every room."

"Felt like I was opening a time capsule. Don't think anyone has been up here in quite a while, well, except for Ruby." He walked toward the largest bedroom at the front of the house with her following. "I thought I'd take this room for a bedroom. It has the best view and may be a little larger than the others." He opened the door and allowed her to enter ahead of him.

"Nice," she said glancing around. "It's over the

study and part of the porch so it'll be quiet, not that I make a lot of noise in my bedroom."

The thought of her having noisy sex made him frown. He hadn't thought about her and other men. Now that he did, he didn't like it.

"What'd I say?" she asked with a crinkled brow. "Why are you frowning at me?"

"Nothing," he said with a shake of his head. "I think all the dust and dirt is giving me a headache," he lied. "I didn't think about this being the quietest room, but you're probably right. C'mon. I need to show you something else."

She followed him into the antiquated bathroom. The old pedestal sink and clawfoot tub were in remarkably good condition. The toilet was showing some age but still, for something nearly fifty years old, it looked surprisingly usable.

"Well," she said, looking around. "My downstairs bathroom looks like it had a renovation compared to this one, although this one has a whole lot more character." She walked over and turned on the cold tap at the sink. Nothing happened.

"No water," he said. "In fact, I don't think water has ever been turned on up here. Looks to me like the Fitzgeralds had plans for a large family. Since they never had kids, I assume they shut this area off since it wasn't needed."

"Think you can just turn on the water and everything will work?"

"If only," he said with a laugh. "No, I think I'd better get a real plumber out here to check everything before we do that. Could be a broken pipe in the wall or something. What a mess that'd be."

"True," she answered, her eyes wide with realization. "I didn't think about that when I turned everything back on. Crap. That could have been a disaster."

"I think Travis and Caroline have been keeping an eye on things, but as long as I'm bringing in a plumber anyway, I'll have him check out the downstairs. To be honest, that half-bath in the back bedroom has a toilet leak that'll have to be fixed. The floor's a little rotten around the ring."

She followed him back into the open area. "Are you going to be using the other bedrooms?"

He shrugged. "Don't know. Haven't thought that far."

Glancing down at her watch, she swore. "I've got to go. My last night of work at Leo's starts in thirty minutes." She hurried toward the stairs. "Good luck with the cleaning," she tossed over her shoulder.

He crossed his arms over his chest. "What? You aren't going to help me?"

"Nope." Her answer floated up from the bottom of the stairs. "You're on your own with that." She produced a fake sneeze. "Dust allergy, remember?"

"Bull," he yelled back. Her answering laugh made him smile.

He didn't deserve her friendliness. He'd treated her horribly. He knew it. Hell, he'd known back then that he was a shit but he hadn't been ready for someone like her in his life.

And now here she was…the right age, the right maturity, the right everything, except this time, he was nothing but a damaged cowboy who had nothing to offer someone like her. She deserved better than him.

After her car crunched down the gravel drive, he headed downstairs to look for cleaning supplies, which he located under the kitchen sink. A new-looking vacuum stood in the hall closet, but he thought a rag with soap and water might do as well.

With no water available, he had to trudge up the steps carrying a three-gallon bucket of soapy water with a stack of cleaning cloths under his arm. Starting in his bedroom, he made a long swipe with a wet cloth down the wall. Years of grime coated his towel.

Maybe he should have hired a cleaning service instead.

Except he needed the exercise. He had to get this done before he could move in here. Once he got finished today, he'd head out for the whiskey he really wanted. Sort of payment for a job well done. Nothing wrong with that.

Two hours later, his left leg was on fire. His back cramped like he'd been on a bull for an hour. Sweat dripped down his face and stung his eyes. But his bedroom was clean.

He stood back, propped his hands on his hips and admired his work. The oak floor gleamed. The glass in the window sparkled. Even the overhead light seemed brighter.

Bending over at his waist, he stretched his hands toward the floor, straightening his back muscles, relieving a little of the pain. His leg still protested bearing his weight for the extended time, but the fire in his thigh had abated a little.

He debated stopping versus moving on to the bathroom and ultimately moved on. If he quit now, he might never get going again.

But, damn, he wanted a beer. Or whiskey. Or a shot of whiskey dropped in a beer.

The bathroom cleaning seemed to go faster. Either because it hadn't collected as much dust over the years—which he doubted—or because he had his cleaning routine down to a fine art—which was where he laid his money. A mere ninety minutes in that room and he was done.

Still, the three-and-a-half hours of cleaning had taken almost five hours when he factored in dumping the dirty water and getting fresh every thirty minutes or so.

He thought about tackling the other rooms, but his phone rang as soon as he picked up his pail of dirty water. Setting it back down, he pulled his phone out of his front pocket.

"Hello?"

"Hi, honey," his mother said. "How are you?"

His knees practically groaned in relief when he sat on the top step to take the call. "I'm good, Mom. What's up?"

"Are you sure you don't want to come stay with us? We loved having you and Noah here the other night."

"I know. But I just…well…"

"Need to do this yourself, right?"

Thankful he'd been given a great set of parents, he smiled. "Something like that."

"The reason I'm calling is that Caroline is coming home from the hospital today or tomorrow. Olivia and I are taking dinner over Sunday. Enough for a family meal. We want you there."

"Are Travis and Caroline aware the entire clan will be invading their house? I mean, they will be just getting home."

"It's Caroline's idea. She wants the babies to meet their family before the rest of the world."

He laughed softly. "Travis picked a winner, didn't he?"

"He did. And so will you some day."

Cash didn't say anything. His mother meant well, he knew that, but she still thought of him as a teenager, not a grown man and especially not as a grown man with no real future.

"You still there, honey?"

"Yes. I'll come. What time?"

"Six would be good. And feel free to bring that girl you're living with."

Wow. News spread in his family like water running downhill. Time to squash his mother's matchmaking. While she might have played around in Olivia and Travis's love lives, he didn't need her help with his.

"Mom. You do realize that Paige and I aren't a couple, right? We're just sharing a house for a short time."

"Of course, honey. I just thought it'd be nice if I got to know her a little better."

"Yeah, well, I don't expect her to come tomorrow night."

His mother sighed. "I just want you to be happy."

"I know, Mom, and I love you for that. I'll see you tomorrow night."

PAIGE WOKE EARLY ON SUNDAY MORNING, SURPRISED since she'd worked until midnight. She hadn't seen Cash back in Leo's bar since Travis had led him out three days ago, but she suspected he'd simply taken his drinking elsewhere. He'd been asleep or passed out in his room when she'd gotten home a little after one. The door to his downstairs bedroom was open. A quick peek had revealed Cash lying on top of his covers still fully dressed, snoring like a buzz saw. She'd fought against her desire to remove his boots, maybe even his jeans, and throw a blanket over him. But that wasn't how he needed to be handled. He had to find his own strength again.

She'd shut the door and gone to her room.

As coffee brewed, she read through her list of household projects that needed to be done. Granted, this was a rental, but she'd tripped four times on that wonky back step. Today was the day it was going to be hammered into place.

When Angus Fitzgerald died and Caroline opted to leave everything in the house, that included a limited set of tools. Paige had found them in a shed out back. As soon as she finished breakfast, she got dressed in jeans and a T-shirt and headed out to find a hammer and hopefully some nails.

She crossed her fingers her plan would work.

She aligned the hole in the board with the hole in the wooden tread where the previous nail had been, deciding that might work. But she found it hard to hold the board in place, the nail upright and then strike it with the hammer.

Bam! Bam!

"Shit," she muttered as the nail bent sideways.

She tapped the side of the nail a couple of times to make it sort of straight again. Lining up the hammer with the nail, she pounded.

Bam! Bam!

The nail bent again.

"Shit." She hit the nail to straighten it.

She lifted the hammer again, but before she could swing it down, the back door flew open.

"What the hell is going on out here?"

Paige lowered the hammer and looked up. The first thing in her vision was two bare feet. The worn hem of a pair of washed-out jeans brushed the tops of the toes. She allowed her gaze to feast on the legs filling out those jeans until she reached a partially closed zipper and an unbuttoned waistband. The dance of a billion butterflies took off in her gut. She swallowed hard while her gaze mentally licked the valleys and swales of a sculpted abdomen. When she finally coasted up his chest and across his muscular crossed arms, she stared into a set of sky-blue eyes. A deep-set frown wrinkled Cash's brow.

"What are you doing?" His voice sounded tired and frustrated.

"Sorry. Did I wake you up? I was trying to fix this step. I tripped over it again last night." She wiggled the board. "It's a little loose."

He studied her and then the board. "It's not loose. It's rotten." He held out his hand. "Give me that hammer."

"But…"

He sighed. "Don't argue. Hand it over."

She did.

"Now go do something else. I'll fix this," he said.

Standing, she brushed the dirt off the knees of her jeans. "Fine. I think I'll go to church."

"Sounds a like an excellent idea."

When she got to the door, she thought he'd step away so she could enter. He didn't. She had enough room to squeeze through into the kitchen, but it required rubbing against him as she passed. Touching him—even through her clothes—made the area between her thighs heat.

She walked away, a grin twitching at her lips. Devious, yes, but—she glanced over her shoulder long enough to see Cash studying the steps—he was up and he had something to do.

Coddling wasn't what he needed. He needed tough love and something to occupy his time.

Once she'd finished dressing for church, she headed to the kitchen to retrieve her purse and keys. She found Cash sitting at the small dining table, his hands wrapped around a cup of coffee.

"Well, I'm off. Not sure when I'll be back," she said.

He grunted his response…whatever it was.

"Later."

"Uh-huh," he said, lifting his coffee.

Cash's family took up the majority of two pews at church. Between the husbands and wives and now growing children, it wouldn't be long before they would spill onto a third pew in the small Methodist church.

Paige found a seat a few rows behind them and slid in. She could see where Cash got his physique and coloring. His father, Lane, was tall and muscular. Obviously a man who did physical labor and, by the deep tan on his neck, did it outdoors. His hair was silver and she wondered if Cash's blond locks would someday look like his father's.

His mother, Jackie, was a tall, striking woman with blonde hair and blue eyes. Her laugh was loud and infectious. It was rare to not see a smile on Jackie Montgomery's face.

His sister, Olivia, was here with her husband, Mitch, and their two kids. Adam, the oldest, had wiggled in to sit between Lane and Jackie and Paige suspected the kid had both his grandparents wrapped around his little finger. When Jackie pulled a coloring book and pack of crayons from her purse and handed them to Adam, Paige couldn't suppress the smile. She didn't know Olivia and her family well, having only interacted in passing, but Olivia never failed to be warm and gracious.

Cash's brother, Jason, sat with his fiancée, Dr. Lydia Henson. Paige knew Lydia better than she knew Jason. Since Paige had settled in Whispering Springs following her parents' deaths, she'd gotten to know Lydia through her friendship with Caroline Graham, Lydia's medical-practice partner. As of tomorrow, Paige would be employed by Whispering Springs Medical Clinic so she was sure she'd get to know Lydia much better.

Paige's insides clenched at the thought of work tomorrow. She was excited and scared to death. Caroline was so positive Paige would be an excellent addition to the clinic staff. She hoped—prayed—she didn't let Caroline down.

Caroline and Travis weren't in attendance today. But then, delivering twins only a couple of days prior would make any couple want to sleep in on a Sunday morning. She wondered when Caroline and the babies would be coming home. When she'd visited at the hospital, both the newborns and Caroline appeared to be doing well.

Paige thought of her own dwindling family. Only Leo and Uncle James remained, and while James had recently married after being a widower for fourteen years, he and his new wife were past the baby-making stage. If her family lineage was to continue, it was up to Leo and her. And knowing her brother, it was up to her.

Her gaze swept across the entire Montgomery family filling the pews. Did Cash have any idea how cool it was to have such a large family? And not only a large family, but one that actually liked each other? She didn't think so. If he did, she'd never seen evidence of it. In all the years she'd known him, he'd never spoken about his family to her. Of course, she'd been a child during most of that time and he'd treated her as such.

Or at least he had until she'd turned eighteen. She put that memory out of her head for now. Wrong place. Wrong time.

When the service was over and she was sitting in her car, she considered going home. But the memory of her night with Cash assailed her again and she wasn't sure she wanted to face him just yet. In some ways, she was embarrassed at how she'd basically insisted on dragging him from a bar to her bed. In other ways, she was still hurt at his reaction the next day.

She started her car and pulled from the lot. As though her engine had a mind of its own, the hood turned toward Dallas and the school she was scheduled to start in the fall. She had some career decisions she needed to make—like did she really want to get a nurse practitioner degree? It'd be another year of school. And a grueling year at that. But at least she'd have better job options.

Her bachelor degree in psychology had been fun and interesting while she'd earned it, but it'd left her with very limited career options. All that education in psychology had come in handy while pursuing her bachelor in nursing, but she wanted more out of life than being an office nurse or a psychiatric nurse.

Getting licensure as a nurse practitioner could open up new career paths.

On the other hand, growing up she'd always thought she might follow in her father's footsteps and go to veterinary school. She could revisit that idea.

Or she could do neither and go back to work at Leo's bar. But there was no future there for sure.

All those thoughts and arguments rattled through her brain and gave her a headache. She didn't want to think about all that today. Instead, her mind dropped into the most memorable night of her life…painful but unforgettable.

It was her eighteenth birthday. Since most of their immediate friends would be riding in a rodeo early that evening, her parents had thrown a big brunch and invited everybody in their rodeo world. Hamburgers, hot dogs, pancakes, omelets, breakfast meats of all kinds, biscuits and, of course, the requisite huge cake with eighteen candles.

The minute Cash Montgomery walked around the front end of her parents' motorhome and smiled, she forgot anyone else was there. He hugged her. Wished her a happy birthday. Winked as he told her that when he won the silver buckle tonight, it was hers. She squealed with delight and then winced at how juvenile it had sounded.

Then he gave her a short, sweet kiss. She wanted more. Wanted to throw her arms around his neck and pull him into a duel of tongues and a mashing of lips.

But her parents were standing there and, as it was her party, the attention was on her. Still, she doubted anyone realized her legs were melting from that chaste kiss or were aware of the lovesick cow eyes she was sure she wore.

Just as he'd promised, Cash won that night. After the rodeo, the cowboys and their women headed to a bar to celebrate Cash's win, with him being the biggest celebrator. She was too young to get in, but that didn't stop her. Well-applied make-up, cowboy boots, a short mini-skirt and a low-cut top, combined with a truly awesome fake driver's license, and she was through the door. She wasn't interested in the alcohol. It was the music and the dancing, not to mention a long-legged, shaggy-haired bull rider who could toss back a whiskey like no one she'd ever seen.

She finagled her way through the crowd until she wedged herself into his group and next to him. Either the others standing there didn't recognize her with the excessive make-up she wore or they didn't care. Focused on their own partying, they paid her little attention. When he finally asked her to dance, she was delirious with teenage glee. She maintained enough composure to just nod and not throw herself at him as an answer.

It was a slow dance…a really slow, really long dance. She was positive he could feel her heart kicking like a bronco against his chest when he held her close. She pressed against his hard body…all her soft places seeming to fit perfectly with his hard ones. His thick thighs rubbed hers, almost sending her to her knees.

Her mouth fit just below his ear. She licked his ear

lobe and followed that by nuzzling her nose against his neck and moving her mouth back to his ear.

"Know what I want for my birthday, cowboy?" she whispered.

He chuckled, his warm breath blowing in her ear and down her neck. "Yes, I know."

Shivering in response, she pulled her arm from around his neck and slipped it between their bodies. There she tugged on his new silver buckle. His lips curled upward on the skin of her neck, followed by a sigh.

"I know. My buckle."

"Then you'd be wrong. It's not the buckle I want. It's what below."

He stilled even though the music was still playing.

"You heard me right, Cash. I want you. I want you to make love to me."

"Paige, honey—"

"No," she whispered back. "You want it too. I felt it in your kiss this morning."

"I've been drinking."

"I haven't. Are you drunk?"

"No, but—"

"I know what I'm doing, what I want."

He pulled back and looked into her eyes. "Are you sure this is what you want?"

She wanted to pump her fist in the air in victory. But she maintained a grown-up facial expression—although she wasn't sure if she really did or if her smile told all. "I'm sure."

He nodded and took her hand. Without a word to

anyone else, they left and headed back to her small trailer, the one her parents had given her when she'd finished high school at age seventeen.

They drove separate trucks back to the camp ground and Cash parked his near his campsite. When he got out, he stood still for a minute, and she feared he'd changed his mind during the drive back. But when she waved at him, he came to her.

What she remembered was the vision of a warrior storming across the park toward her. The moon at his back. The incredible breadth and strength in his shoulders as he neared. A confident strut to his stride. He was everything she wanted. Everything she'd ever wanted since she'd first laid eyes on him at age fourteen.

He followed her into her small living area. As soon as the door shut, he backed her against it, trapping her between his hard body and an equally hard door. Sexual voltage ricocheted through her. As soon as his lips touched hers, she opened her mouth, giving him access. He licked and drank from her, swirled and dipped and stroked with his tongue, rubbed his cock against her stomach, and she responded with a low moan into his mouth.

She slipped her hand between them like she had on the dance floor, but this time she didn't bother with the buckle. Who cared about a buckle when he had something she wanted so much more. She grasped his rigid length through his jeans, rippling her fingers up and down.

He broke the kiss long enough to jerk her top over

her head. He moved his mouth to her breast and captured her flesh through her lace bra. She arched into his kiss. His hot breath and talented tongue drew her nipple to painfully erect within seconds. Closing his teeth around the tip, he nibbled and licked until she was crazy with desire.

He skated his hands down her body until he held both globes of her ass in his palms. He squeezed her flesh at the same time he bit down on her nipple. She groaned. She'd had no idea sensations like these existed.

Cool air had chill bumps rising on her thighs as he pushed her skirt to her waist. She ground her thong-covered mons on his stiff shaft, her sex throbbing with a demanding need.

He stroked his hands down to the back of her thighs. His biceps bulged when he hoisted her up against her door as though she weighed nothing.

"Put your legs around me," he ordered.

She did, her now-wet thong pressed directly against his bulging zipper. He walked toward her tiny bedroom, which with his long legs took only three strides.

He laid her on the bed, his massive frame looming over her. Her clothing melted away under his talented fingers. The first time she felt his hot flesh on hers, all the stars in her world aligned. Nothing had ever felt so good, so right.

His reputation with women was nothing like the real man. It didn't begin to describe the sensations and outright heights he drove her to as he covered her body with his lips, his tongue, his hands. Stroking. Caressing. Kissing. Licking. He never stopped. She could hardly draw a breath.

He drove her to the brink but not beyond. She clutched the sheets, begged him for something, even though she had no idea what she was begging him to do. His first thrust into her had made her gasp. The pain from the foreign intrusion inside her stunned her momentarily. By the fourth, her eyes rolled back in her head in pleasure. When she finally flew over the rim, her body responded with quakes and ripples.

"I love you," she said. "I've loved you forever."

He didn't move. Not a thrust. Not a breath. She felt his heart throbbing rapidly against her chest.

He thrust one more time and then pulled out. He kissed her forehead and went into her tiny bathroom.

That might have been her first time, but her dad had been a veterinarian. She'd been raised around animals. Knew all about reproduction. She knew about the male penis be it on a horse, cow or man. She knew about ejaculate and she knew, beyond a shadow of a doubt, Cash Montgomery had not come.

Emotionally crushed, she pulled the sheet up to her chin, He was disappointed. She wasn't good enough or sexy enough for him. He'd had a lot of women and it was obvious she'd not met his expectations. She wanted to die.

When the bathroom door reopened, he wore a scowl and quickly redressed. Once his jeans were fastened, he pulled the belt out of the loops and placed it on top of her bed.

"I promised you this."

"No, Cash. You should keep it."

He shook his head. "No. A promise is a promise."

He left and she dissolved into tears.

The next time she saw him, he had his left arm around a blonde and his right around a brunette. Both women were well-known and well-used buckle bunnies, women who followed the rodeo for a chance to sleep with a real-live cowboy. He nodded to her and then tightened his hold on his escorts.

For the next month, she saw him with a different woman, or set of women, every time their paths crossed. She cried herself to sleep every night, not having a clue what had gone wrong. Had she been so bad in bed he couldn't wait to leave?

Her parents kept asking what was wrong. "Nothing," she said most of the time. Sometimes she threw in, "Just bored," to keep them off the scent of her misery.

During a late-night discussion and cry session with Leo, she told him everything, except the name of the cowboy. As she told him, it didn't matter what his name was. She was done with him and with cowboys. It was Leo who convinced her to go to college.

That fall she enrolled in Pepperdine University, figuring she'd see more sand and surfers than cowboys. And she did. But she missed the dirt, the smell of horse and cattle, her tiny trailer. She missed her old life and her parents, but even after she earned a bachelor degree in psychology from Pepperdine, she still didn't feel prepared for life, and realistically, for a job.

So it was on to California State University in Long Beach for a bachelor degree in nursing, intending to continue her education at the graduate level.

Her parents came for her CSU graduation, driving all the way from Wyoming. They toured all over California, up and down the Pacific Coast Highway more times than she could count. With their support, she was ready to take on the world—even a world where Cash Montgomery lived.

And then on a road trip to Northern California, her parents died in a fiery car crash, leaving her alone and devastated.

Her world shattered into a billion tiny shards, and she was still putting the pieces of her life back together today. Who would help her sweep up the rubble if Cash destroyed that fragile world again?

Chapter Five

Cash finished his coffee before heading out to look at the steps, which only confirmed his original opinion. The step didn't need to be repaired. The entire staircase was falling apart and needed to be replaced.

With Travis scheduled to bring home his wife and babies, Cash hesitated calling, but this place wasn't his. There was no sense in spending money making repairs if Travis didn't want him to, so he called. His brother answered on the first ring.

"Cash? Is there a problem?"

Cash bit back the cuss word on the tip of his tongue. That was his older brother's reaction to all Cash's calls. *What has little brother done now?*

"Nothing major's wrong," he said after regaining control of his temper. "I need to do a little work on the back steps. Well, actually, I need to replace the back steps to the porch. They've gotten a little soft."

"Fine. Whatever you need to do," he said, sounding distracted and winded.

"Great. Didn't want to make changes without your knowledge."

Travis huffed into the phone.

"What are you doing?" Cash asked.

"Sorry. Running late. I'm trying to dress and talk to you at the same time. Caroline is really attached to that house. Anything that needs fixing, feel free and send me the bill."

"Okay, big bro. That's what I'll do. See you tonight."

"Tonight? Right. Family dinner." The sound of a door slamming resounded through the phone.

"Go bring your family home."

"I am. Right now. Hey, Cash."

"What?"

"Can you believe I have two kids? And a wife?"

The bit of anger still inside Cash winked out and he chuckled at the giddy astonishment in his brother's voice. It'd been a long time since he'd heard his brother sound so happy. No, not happy. More like sky-high elated. He was thrilled for Travis, but privately, maybe he had a blush of envy. His brother had it all. "You'll be a great dad. See you tonight."

Cash drove an hour to one of the large chain lumber stores, knowing that nothing would be open in Whispering Springs on a Sunday morning. That was one of the problems with small towns. Inaccessibility to essentials when needed, regardless of what the needed essential might be.

Three hours later, and a couple of hundred dollars poorer, he pulled back up to Singing Springs ranch, the backend of his truck loaded with fresh lumber, screws, a new power saw and a few other odds and ends. Loading the heaving boards had strained his left leg and it had throbbed painfully on the drive back.

As he pulled the wood from the truck, he thought of Paige and how cute she'd looked trying to drive a crooked nail into a board. Good thing she was book-smart. House construction didn't appear to have been part of her college education.

Of course, he knew all about her college degrees, her grades, her awards. Hell, everybody chasing the white line who'd spent more than five minutes with her parents knew all that. They'd been so proud of her.

Paige was smart and beautiful, a deadly combination. She needed to get out of this backwater town and move to Dallas or Fort Worth or Austin, somewhere more cosmopolitan, to a city where all the smart adults lived. She had nothing tying her to Whispering Springs but a dead-end job at Leo's Bar and Grill and why she was working there made no sense at all.

He dropped the first board on the ground and remembered kissing Paige when she'd been sixteen. He'd been twenty. Too old and too experienced for someone her age. In fact, the cowboys had called her Doc Ryan's jail bait.

The kiss at her eighteenth birthday party had zapped him like a stun gun. And even though at eighteen she'd no longer legally qualified as jail bait, he'd still felt too old and way too jaded for someone as sweet as she. He'd backed away, promising her—and himself—that he'd win the silver buckle that night just for her. And he had.

After unloading the lumber, he leaned on the truck's tailgate to rub his leg. The vision of Paige strutting into the bar on the night of her eighteenth birthday played in his mind. She'd looked older, more mature and definitely twenty-one. If she'd ordered a drink, he'd have taken her home to her parents immediately, but she'd seemed more interested in dancing than drinking, and there was no harm in that.

The other cowboys had all taken a turn with her on the floor, but she'd only accepted fast dances from them. When he'd asked her to dance, a slow country love song had played and she'd allowed him to lead her to the floor.

That had been his first mistake. Fast music that didn't require that he actually touch her would have been miles safer.

Pulling her softness against him had made him so hard he'd feared zipper tread marks on his dick. When she'd kissed his ear and told him that she wanted to sleep with him, he should have said no. Not that he wasn't attracted to her and flattered as shit. Hell, what cowboy in his right mind wouldn't have been. Truth to tell, he'd probably been a little more than simply attracted to her back then. Maybe still was, not that it would do him any good today.

Even back then she'd deserved better than him. Had he not been drinking, his shields to her charms would have fully engaged. Instead, his alcohol-fueled decision-making abilities had thought fucking sounded like a great idea. The way she'd licked his ear and so plainly stated her desires had made him realize that her proposition for sex couldn't have been her first time.

For a brief moment, he'd wanted to find the bastard who'd taken her virginity and kill him. It was only later that he'd realized who the bastard was he needed to kill, and he'd damned near succeeded in doing just that.

The drive back to the camp ground had given him time to reflect and come to the conclusion that making love to Paige Ryan was a bad idea. Ready to back off with the excuse of too much booze, he'd seen her in the moonlight, her gold hair strands woven in among the red ones, and he'd gone weak in the knees. He'd had trouble drawing breath, much less a voice to beg off. She'd waved and he'd gone like a bull at a red cape.

That first kiss inside her trailer had been his undoing. He'd wanted her for so long, had fantasized about this night, he could barely restrain his primitive urge to take her fast and hard against her door. It had taken an iron will to restrain himself long enough to get her onto her bed.

Her flesh had been soft and sweet. Her moans and sighs had fired up his insides to an inferno. Her fingers grasping her sheets, her arched back pressing into him had almost made him come like a thirteen-year-old boy with a *Playboy* magazine.

But when he'd finally, finally thrust inside, his heart had swelled so large he could barely breathe. She'd been his undoing. She was so tight, a velvet-lined fist grabbing his cock and squeezing it. He'd had to fight his immediate urge to come. It hadn't taken much to send Paige into an orgasm. He couldn't remember ever having a partner so responsive to him, so in tune to his touches.

And then she'd told him she loved him.

His heart had almost stopped. He knew his breathing had.

Too young and too sheltered to know what she really felt, she hadn't begun to experience life outside the rodeo circuit, and no way did their lives reflect the normal world. She deserved more…the big house, the white picket fence, a husband who adored her, the requisite two or three children. He could give her none of these things.

He was too rough for someone as sweet and gentle as Paige. He'd been nothing more than a cowboy who could hold onto a rope and ride an angry bull. She had too much potential to tie herself to someone like that.

In that instant, he'd decided it wouldn't happen again, they couldn't happen again, no matter what it took. He'd tried to fake an orgasm, still unsure to this day if she'd bought it. The one thing he had been sure of was he had to get out of there before he whispered those three words back to her, because that would have killed her future, and he wouldn't do that to her.

Leaving her that night had taken every ounce of steel he could muster. He'd have rather gone to hell than hurt her. In some ways, that wish had come true. Seeing her, pretending to enjoy the company of buckle bunnies day after day had been his own personal hell.

Hating their past, hating that he knew he'd hurt her, he took his anger out on the rotten wood, destroying the treads, the risers and the stringers along the sides until there was nothing left. Then he got to work on a new set of steps.

The saw whined to a stop, the small end of the board dropping to the ground. Tires crunching on the drive gravel echoed around to the back of the house. He heard a car door slam and then gravel crunching again as the car drove away. Cash paused, waiting to see who'd come to check on him. It kind of pissed him off that his family felt like he needed to be looked after.

He grabbed a handful of screws and set to attaching the step to the raiser. No one came around the corner. He paused to listen. A dog's whimper came from the front of the house. Frowning, he headed in that direction.

In the drive facing the road sat a small brown dog with floppy ears. When Cash stepped onto the gravel, the puppy's head whipped toward him.

"Hey, buster. Who are you?"

He lowered into a squat, wincing at the pain in his

leg, and held out his hand. The puppy cowered, his shoulder hunched up and his head lowered.

Anger ignited into Cash. Some sonofabitch had beaten this puppy and dumped him.

"You're okay," he said in a gentle voice. "Come here." He continued to hold out his hand. The puppy took a couple of steps toward him but it was plain to see the animal was terrified.

Cash stood. The dog shied away.

"It's okay," he said again. "Nobody's going to hurt you."

Approaching the dog with slow, measured steps, he was able to get close enough to touch the puppy's head. After stroking down the dog's back a couple of times, the animal appeared to be sufficiently calmed to allow Cash to pick him up. The poor thing shook violently in his arms.

He carried the puppy into the house to the kitchen, filled a bowl with water and watched as the animal lapped as though he were dying of thirst. While standing, the dog held his left rear leg off the ground.

Poor guy was hurt. If he could find the bastards who had hurt this dog and dumped him, Cash would make them feel as miserable as this little guy felt. He needed to get the puppy to a veterinarian to see if that leg was broken. But damn if it wasn't Sunday.

He called his sister. After all, she had a dog. Maybe she could take this one too.

"Morning, Olivia."

"Morning, little bro. When you coming to our house for dinner?"

The picture of that satanic baby bull at the entrance to Olivia's ranch flashed in his mind. God, he hated bulls. He was going to have to deal with Mitch and their joint business one day, but not today.

"I don't know. Soon. Listen, I need some help. Some bastard dumped a puppy at my front door a little while ago. He looks hurt. Are we still using Mabee as our vet?"

"Yep, but he's not back yet from his honeymoon. Dr. Brian is covering. It'll be the end of the week before Mabee is back. Call Dr. Brian. He'll meet you at the clinic." She gave him the phone number.

As she predicted, Dr. Brian told Cash to bring the puppy on by and to use the rear door to get in the clinic.

There were times Cash hated being a Montgomery, like when his parents would get anonymous phone calls telling them, "I saw Cash smoking," or "I saw Cash drinking," or "Saw Cash drag racing out on Strawberry Hill Road." But then there were times, like now, when being a Montgomery had its benefits.

A beat-up Ford truck was backed in behind Whispering Springs Animal Hospital. Cash parked and carried the still-shaking dog into the building. Getting the puppy into his truck had been a problem. The poor thing had cried as soon as Cash had set him on the seat. The sorrowful wailing had broken his heart but strengthened his resolve to find this guy a good home. Maybe the vet would know of someone looking.

Dr. Brian was an older man, well past the retirement age. White-haired. Wrinkled face. Thick glasses. But his eyes softened as soon as he saw the pup.

"Thanks for meeting me," Cash said.

"Glad to, son. At my age, it's good to have something to do."

Cash set the shivering puppy on the exam table. "I don't know anything about him. Some sonofabitch—sorry, Doc—some person dropped him at my house."

"I agree with you," the older man said, his eyes taking on a hard stare. "I hate people who dump animals." He stroked down the dog's back. "Hey, little guy. What's going on?" His voice was gentle and calming and the puppy responded to the tone enough that the shaking slowed.

The doctor listened to the dog's heart, drew blood, took a fecal sample and performed an examination. When he left the room to run the lab tests, Cash picked up the puppy and held him in his lap until the doctor returned.

"Well?" Cash asked.

"All in all, he's pretty healthy. No heartworms. Heart sounds good."

"What about his leg? Why is he limping and holding it off the ground?"

"It's not broken. I think we're looking at a ligament strain. He'll be fine in a few days. While you're here, we should go ahead and do his vaccinations and license."

"But I can't keep him," Cash protested. "Don't you know anyone who's looking for a dog?"

The vet shook his head. "Sorry, no. You can take him to the county pound. He might be adopted from there."

"And if he isn't?"

Dr. Brian hesitated.

"They'd kill him, right?"

The vet shrugged. "It's sad, but we have a huge overpopulation of unwanted cats and dogs. There's only so many that are adopted or can be cared for."

Cash pulled the dog closer. "I'm not letting some SOB kill this puppy after all he's been through. Go ahead and give him all the shots. I'll find him a good home."

"Okay. I can do that. Does he have a name?"

Cash looked down at the puppy that was looking up at him with large brown eyes. "Buster."

By the time Cash and Buster got back into his truck, Buster had a new collar, leash, license, rabies tag, puppy chow, bowls, heartworm medicine, a dog crate and an orthopedic dog bed, and Cash was four-hundred dollars poorer.

It'd been an expensive Sunday and the day wasn't over yet.

When he drove down the Singing Springs drive, he was surprised that Paige hadn't made it home from church yet, not that he cared one way or the other.

He and Buster parked at the rear of the house. As Cash took up where he'd left off in his stair rebuild,

Buster played in the yard, never venturing far from Cash.

He worked until four-thirty, leaving himself plenty of time to put away all the tools and get a shower before heading to Travis and Caroline's for dinner. Buster remained affixed to Cash's side. When he moved, the puppy moved. What was he going to do with Buster while he was gone tonight?

He scooped up the dog and headed for the shower. Both of them needed one, so not to waste the water, Cash decided to do both of them at one time. When they got out, he borrowed a couple of clean towels from Paige's stash, drying Buster and then himself quickly. He'd hoped if he waited long enough, Paige would get home and keep an eye on Buster, if she wasn't too pissed about the puppy. He'd make sure she understood the dog was just temporary.

By five-forty-five, he had to leave and Paige still wasn't home.

"Well, Buster. How'd you like to meet my family?"

The puppy licked Cash's chin. No way was this guy going to the pound.

He rolled up to Halo M ranch at six p.m. as instructed. Travis and his first wife, Susan, had built a large classical Southern ranch house with white pillars and a wraparound porch. After Susan died, Travis had stayed in the house, and even though he'd told the entire world he'd never marry again, Cash was happy for his brother that he'd found Caroline Graham.

The front door opened before Cash could get out

of his truck. His sister-in-law stood in the doorway, a newborn in one arm and a bright smile on her face.

"Come on in," she said.

"Am I the last one here?"

"Nope. Still waiting on Jason and Lydia. Who's that with you?"

"This is Buster." Cash gave her a peck on the cheek. "You are looking great. How do you feel?"

"Thanks. I feel like a won a lottery." She looked at the dog. "Buster?"

"I hope you don't mind. I didn't know what else to do with him and I didn't want to cancel. Someone dumped him at Singing Springs today and he's just so young and scared."

"I don't mind. How old is he?"

"The vet says about three months." He followed Caroline into the house carrying the dog in his arms. "You want a puppy?"

She shut the door behind them and laughed before giving him a hug. "Nope."

"Hey!" Travis boomed as he walked to the front door. "That's my woman. Get your own."

Cash laughed. "You married down," he told Caroline.

"I know," she said with a grin. "But what could I do? He knocked me up."

Travis slung his arm around his wife and leaned over to nuzzle the baby's head. "Best thing I ever did."

Caroline rolled her eyes. "The rest of the family is in the living room. Your mom and Olivia are in the kitchen. They won't let me step a foot in there."

The aroma of yeast rolls wafted down the hall.

"Mom made rolls?" When Travis nodded, Cash slapped him on the back. "I've been craving those."

"Who's this?" Travis asked as he and Cash walked away leaving Caroline talking to Olivia's husband, Mitch.

"This is Buster. He's temporary," Cash said. "Dumped at the house today. He was so scared, I couldn't leave him alone."

Travis rubbed the dog's long, floppy ears. "Looks like he's got some hound in him."

"You want him? He needs to find a home."

Travis answered with a loud laugh. "Sorry. Two new babies. Remember?"

Cash followed Travis to the makeshift bar in the family room.

"What can I get you?" Travis asked.

"Crown and Coke."

Travis turned away to fix the drink and then handed a glass with ice and a still-bubbling soft drink to Cash.

He took a sip. "I think you forgot something."

"No, I didn't," Travis answered.

Cash narrowed his eyes. "I asked for Crown and Coke."

"You don't need Crown."

Cash sat his drink on the bar, trying to reign in his rising temper. "You don't get to say what I need. I don't have to give up booze just because you were too weak to handle it."

Travis took a sip of his diet soda. "Do you think

for one second that I would have a wife like Caroline and two children if I'd kept on swimming in that bottle? Of course not. I didn't decide to give up booze. I decided to live. You're not an alcoholic, Cash. Not yet. But, baby brother, you're on your way."

Cash's flash-fire temper roared to life, but before he could say anything, his other brother stepped up, probably to give him a little more hell. Wasn't that what older brothers were good for? Harassing younger brothers?

"What are we talking about over here?" Jason asked. "You both look a little tense."

"Nothing important," Cash said.

At the same time, Travis said, "Cash's drinking problem."

Cash glared at him. "I don't have a problem."

Jason shrugged. "I don't know, Cash. You were pretty bad the other night."

Cash wheeled to face him. "That was one night, damn it. One fucking night."

"Not from the reports we heard along your trek home from the hospital," Jason said.

"What? Did you have spies in every bar between here and Las Vegas?"

"Didn't need to. The tabloids did a pretty good job documenting most of your drunken benders."

The loud, harsh exchange between the brothers had the dog shaking. Nuzzling against Cash's forearm, Buster pushed his head under Cash's elbow and into his armpit.

Mitch Landry stepped up on Cash's other side,

five-month-old Eliza Grace Landry cuddled in his arms. "Getting a little loud over here, and my little girl doesn't like it. Looks like the puppy doesn't either. Do I need to referee?"

Travis shook his head. "Nope. I was just explaining to Cash how lucky I am to have Caroline as my wife… not to mention two awesome kids."

Mitch nuzzled the top of Eliza Grace's head. "I know. I can't believe Olivia and I have two now." He looked at Jason. "When are you and Lydia stepping up to the plate?"

"Good question," Cash said, glad to have the discussion off him. He ran his hand down Buster's back in long strokes. "It's okay," he cooed. "No reason to be scared." He glanced toward Jason. "Where is she anyway?"

"She was on call, so she stayed at home. Plus, she felt like this was for family so…"

"Awww," Cash said. "Trouble in Loverville?"

"No." Jason picked up the drink Travis had placed in front of him. "We're fine."

"Hmm," Travis said. "How long have you two been together? Four years? Six?"

"Five."

"And engaged what? A year? Two years?"

Jason shrugged. "Maybe a little over two years. Why?"

The three other men exchanged glances.

"What?" Jason said.

"You may not realize it yet, but you've got a problem."

"No, I don't." Jason puffed out a disgusted sigh. "Lydia just wanted to wait until her practice was established."

"How about another drink?" Lane Montgomery said as he joined his sons.

"Sure, Pop," Travis said, reaching for another liter of regular Coke on a shelf under the bar.

"This is Buster," Cash said before his dad could ask. "I'm trying to find a home for him. You looking for a pup?"

His dad shook his head. "Nice looking hound but nope. Not looking."

"Austin wants to join all the other Montgomery men," Caroline said, handing a wrapped newborn to her husband. "Oh, and of course Miss Eliza Grace. Speaking of which, where is Adam?"

"Home with Magda. They had big plans for pizza and Disney movies."

Caroline grinned. "Do you want to put him to bed? Or I can," she said, extending her hands.

"I'll do it," Travis said, snuggling the bundle close to his chest.

She shrugged. "Go for it. If I can get Britney away from your mother, I'll put her down too."

Cash watched the interaction between Travis and his wife and the way his brother clasped his son tightly to his chest. Travis was a different man. Calm. Happy. Sober.

For the first time, Cash wondered if his brothers were right…but no. He didn't have a problem with booze. Did he?

Of course not. He'd show them. He could do without booze.

He turned to Mitch. "Now, I don't think I have had the pleasure of being introduced to my new niece."

Mitch unwrapped his daughter to show her off. "This is Eliza Grace Landry. Eliza Grace, this is your Uncle Cash."

Cash slipped the loop of the dog leash over his wrist and set Buster on the floor. He held out his arms and Mitch passed Eliza Grace to him. "Hey, sweetheart. I'm Uncle Cash, the fun uncle, unlike your Uncle Travis and Uncle Jason. They're the mean uncles. I'm the one you come to when you need anything."

Travis laughed. "What he means is, he's the one she'll come to when she gets in trouble."

Jason snorted his agreement.

"Don't you mind them, Eliza Grace." Cash held her tiny body snug against him and let the fresh scent of baby powder fill his senses. That she was so small, so defenseless against all the hurts in the world, made him feel overly protective about the small baby. He remembered Adam at this age. Time was certainly passing.

Or was it that life was passing him by?

He glanced at his brother and then at Mitch. "I feel sorry for the first boys who show up to date your daughters."

Travis shrugged. "Not a problem. Mitch and I have a plan, right?"

Mitch laughed. "Yep. Like the country song says, I'll be sitting on my front porch just cleaning my gun. It'll get a message to the rest of them."

Cash shook his head. "Don't you worry," he told the sleeping infant in his arms. "Your dad will come around."

"Better hand her back," Mitch said, extending his arms. "I promised Olivia I'd put her to bed before we ate."

Over dinner, the conversation turned to Caroline's time off.

"I'm sure Lydia is going to miss you, dear," Jackie said to her daughter-in-law. "How's the temporary doctor working out?"

Caroline shook her head. "He didn't. He wanted to do things differently than how we do. Just couldn't get into our system. He'll be leaving at the end of next week, which is why poor Lydia had call again this weekend."

"What's your long-term plan?" Olivia asked.

"I'm going back to work in eight weeks." Caroline reached over to rub her husband's neck. "And this one's not happy about it."

"That's because you don't have to work," Travis groused.

"I love Whispering Springs Medical Clinic. I love my work. I love the staff. I have wonderful patients. Of course I'm going back to work."

Travis lifted his wife's hand to his lips and kissed her knuckles. "I know and that's the only reason I'm not putting up a fight with you going back. And I know Lydia won't let you work yourself too hard either."

"But that's temporary," Jackie said. "I understand the clinic is drawing patients from out in the rural areas too."

Caroline nodded. "True, but so much of what we see is repetitive problems like upper-respiratory infections or immunizations. We decided to add a nurse practitioner to the staff. We thought about advertising and pulling someone in but we hated moving someone here. If they don't fit or click with the clinic personnel, everybody's got a problem. The person who moved. Us. The staff. But we got lucky this week. You all know Paige Ryan, right? She was accepted into a nurse-practitioner program in Dallas. She's local and determined to make this her home." Caroline looked around the table with a bright smile. "She starts work at the clinic tomorrow. Her classes don't start until the fall so we thought some real-world experience would be beneficial, not to mention we need the help."

Cash choked on the sip of water he'd just taken. "Paige? My Paige?"

"Your Paige?" Travis asked with a lift of his eyebrows.

"No, no. Not like that," Cash hurried to say. He looked at Caroline. "We are talking about the woman I'm sharing Singing Springs with, right?"

"That's right."

"But why would she want to settle in Whispering Springs?"

"To be near her brother, would be my guess," Caroline said.

"Her brother?" Cash's brow furrowed in confusion. "What brother?"

"Leo Mabee," Travis said.

"Leo Mabee? Of Leo's Bar and Grill?" Stunned didn't quite describe Cash's reaction to the news. "She and Leo are siblings?"

"Well," Jackie said, lifting her wine to take a sip before she continued, "as I understand it, Leo is her half-brother. Same mother. Different fathers."

Cash leaned back in his chair. "I had no idea. Wait. Isn't Leo the nephew of James Mabee, our vet?"

Travis nodded. "Yes. James's sister married his best friend from vet school. That'd be Paige's dad."

"How come nobody told me all this?"

A collective shrug went around the table.

"Why would we?" Olivia said. "You were long gone on the PBR circuit when James moved to town. I don't know why Paige's parents didn't mention anything, but do men even talk about stuff like that?"

"Not me, honey," Mitch said, draping his arm on his wife's chair. "Now, if you want to talk cattle breeding, I'm your man. Or sex. I'm your man there too," he said under his breath but loud enough that the ones sitting closest to them heard.

Olivia punched his shoulder with a giggle.

Cash took another drink of water, his mind whirling with implications. Did Leo know about Paige and Cash? And if he did, why hadn't he beaten Cash to a pulp?

"To a different subject," Jackie said, "have any of you met Sheriff Bell's new deputy?"

"I have," Caroline said.

Travis's head whipped toward her. "You have? When?"

"A couple of weeks ago, I guess. His name is Marc Singer. He's been making his way around town meeting people. He came by our place about noon and took Lydia and me to lunch. I think he's hitting all the professionals in town, just meeting and getting to know everyone. I think it's a good idea for us to have a good working relationship with the sheriff's department."

"I hear he's quite good looking." Jackie gave a devilish grin.

"He is," Caroline said then laughed at her husband scowl. "He's tall, dark and handsome. And…" she nudged Travis's shoulder, "…he's single."

"You're taken," he said around a mouth of steak.

She laughed. "You know what I should do? I should introduce him to Paige. I bet they would hit it off."

"Why?" Cash snapped. "What do they have in common? Plus, he's probably too old for her."

"Don't think so," Caroline said, her gaze on him. "He's only about thirty-two or so. I'll have to make a mental note to tell Lydia to introduce them since I won't be in the office for a while."

The conversation moved to the campaign of Sheriff Danny Bell for reelection and how this would probably be his last term. Cash stopped listening.

Thinking about Paige with another man, especially with the two of them sharing a house, had his mother's delicious food tasting a lot like sawdust.

PAIGE WAS ALREADY HOME AND IN HER BEDROOM when Cash rolled in from his brother's house, which was probably a good thing since he hadn't yet told her about Buster. But the puppy was only temporary.

Plus, she had Ruby and they hadn't discussed that, so she shouldn't have a problem with Buster. And since she was probably already asleep, it wouldn't be right to wake her up to tell her about Buster. This would all have to wait until morning.

That she occupied so much of his thoughts made him itchy. She was off-limits…way off-limits. However, the revelations about her at dinner had generated a litany of questions. Since he always saw her at breakfast, he could introduce her to their temporary dog and then ply her with all the questions pinging in his head.

He and Buster made their way to the back bedroom and collapsed into deep sleep. His plan for a breakfast session with his roommate didn't pan out as he'd intended. By the time the puppy woke him up to go outside, it was almost eight a.m. After letting his temporary dog into the backyard, Cash stumbled toward the coffee pot and realized that Paige had already left for work.

He'd never been a morning person and doubted he ever would be. After downing his required cup of joe, he remembered the plumber had an appointment to be there between eight and noon. He hurriedly dressed and was just shoving his feet into boots when he heard the knock at the door.

Two hours later, the plumber had gone. Water flowed to the upstairs bath. Cash could do the work required on the half-bath at some time in the future.

Although he hated leaving Buster alone, he had to go to town. He erected the kennel upstairs in one of the extra rooms, shoved a dog mattress that was nicer than the one he was sleeping on into the cage and locked Buster in. The sad-dog eyes almost had him grabbing Buster's lead, but he stayed firm.

After changing clothes, he headed into Whispering Springs to Hodges Fine Furniture, the only furniture store in town, to find something to sleep on that wasn't a rock-filled mattress. It'd cost more to go there, but it was worth giving his business to a local.

He was surprised to find Paige home when he arrived at four.

"Hey." He gave her his standard greeting, hoping she wouldn't notice the inane grin on his face. "How did the new job go?"

"Hey, yourself. Do I hear a dog whining?"

"Maybe."

"Maybe, my eye. I let him out when I got home. He's in the backyard. Probably about ready to come in. When were you going to tell me you got a dog?"

He shrugged. "I didn't exactly get a dog. Some bastard beat him and dumped him here yesterday. I'm trying to find him a home. And I was going to tell you this morning but you left too early."

"Hmm. That kind of pisses me off. Not you having a dog," she hurried to add. "But at the jerk who would do that to such a cute puppy. The dog have a name?"

"Buster." He started toward the door to let the pup in and stopped. "Ruby and Buster?"

She smiled. "Big buddies."

The relief that flooded his system at her words surprised him. "Good." He opened the back door to find Buster sitting there waiting to come in. "How was work?"

"Great. Loved working with Lydia and the office staff was so nice."

She lowered into a squat and held her hand out to the puppy. Then Cash realized Paige was holding out a piece of a hot dog, which meant Buster dumped him and went immediately to Paige. He couldn't blame the dog. He understood Paige's appeal even when she wasn't holding out a hot dog.

She stood. "I thought I'd cook up a nice dinner to celebrate. Interested?"

"Are you kidding? A dinner that I don't have to make? I'm all over that."

She opened the refrigerator and pulled out a package of meat. "It'll take a couple of hours to cook this roast, but it's still early. We have time."

"Sounds good. Wait." He frowned. "Time for what?"

She turned to face him, resting against the counter.

"To go riding. I checked in on Caroline and the babies today. I mentioned how much I missed riding. Travis called later and invited us over to ride this evening."

Cash didn't say anything. He hadn't been on the back of any living creature in six months.

"It's a horse, Cash. Not a bull."

His spine straightened in offense at her words. Was she implying that he was scared?

"Why not?" he said. "Sounds like fun."

Except it didn't. It sounded like one of the rings of hell.

Dinner in the oven, Paige hustled him to her car. Buster was back in his kennel and Ruby had been secured in Paige's bedroom so not to torture the dog through the bars of his cage.

"I'll drive," she said, opening the driver's door.

"I can drive you know," Cash said in a derisive tone.

"I know, but I'm betting my car is cleaner than your truck."

She had him there. His truck was always in a needing-to-be-cleaned-out state and with the addition of Buster having been in the seat, it might be a little worse than usual. He climbed into the passenger side, deciding that saying nothing was the best answer. Damn, she was right. The floors of her SUV weren't littered with fast-food wrappers, crumpled receipts or even a layer of dirt. Plus, it smelled better than his.

"When was the last time you rode?" he asked.

"Been a while." Paige looked to the left and then pulled onto the road. "I don't have a horse anymore, and it's sort of rude to call people and ask if you can come over and ride their horses."

Cash chuckled. "I guess so. What happened to Lady Jane Grey?"

She gave him a wide-eyed stare. "I can't believe you remember the name of my horse."

Heat radiated up his neck. "Can't imagine why I do either. So, where is she?"

"When I left for college, Uncle James came and got her. Told me he had a great home for her. Broke my heart, but I understood. She was only five so she still had a lot of years left in her. Plus, she so loved being with people. It would have been cruel to just stick her in a pasture."

"Why haven't you tried to find her?"

"It wouldn't be right. It's been seven years. I'm sure the people who have her love her as much as I did."

"Well, Travis has a stable full of horses that need exercise. You're doing him a favor today. Trust me."

"I am so excited." She glanced over at him and smiled. His heart skipped. Her jade-green eyes sparkled with anticipation. "I hope I don't fall off immediately."

He laughed. "I doubt you will."

She turned into the drive and followed Cash's instructions to the stable. When they climbed out, Eli Elliott, one of Travis's cowboys, walked over.

"Hey, Cash. Ma'am." He touched the brim of his hat and gave a dip of his head.

"Eli, my man." Cash and he shook hands. "Been a while."

"Yes, it has. Travis told me you two were coming. I've got a couple of nice ones saddled and ready to go. Both of them need the exercise, so they might be a little frisky."

Cash looked at Paige. "See? Told you so." He looked at Eli. "I told her on the way over that Travis always needs help getting all his horses exercised."

"You got that right. If you'll wait here, I'll be right back."

Shortly, Eli led a grey mare from the barn, saddled and ready to ride. "I believe this one is yours, ma'am."

Paige froze. The color drained from her face, leaving red dots of blush on her cheeks. Her mouth dropped open. She lifted her hand to cover her mouth.

"Oh my God."

Chapter Six

Cash looked over at her when he heard her gasp. Tears trickled down her cheeks. "Paige?"

"Lady Jane Grey?" Paige's heart pounded so hard and so loud in her ears she could barely hear. She took one step forward.

Eli nodded. "Yes, ma'am. That's her name."

She felt the wetness on her face but she couldn't stop. Her uncle had brought her horse here. Lady Jane Grey had been here all along.

"Lady?" she said.

The horse turned her head toward Paige's voice and then stepped in that direction. Paige ran over and threw her arms around the horse's neck.

"Oh my God. I didn't think I'd ever see you again," she said, stroking the horse with long tender touches. "You are beautiful."

"Do you need help getting on?" the cowboy asked.

"Nope." She put her left foot in the stirrup and slipped onto her horse's back like it'd been seven hours since they'd been together instead of seven years. She took the reins and walked her mare around.

Lady Jane Grey was fidgety, shaking her head and neighing loudly. She was ready to run.

"Go on," Cash said. "I'll catch up."

Paige pointed to a tall tree in the distance. "See that pine? I'll see you there."

She tapped gently. "Let's go, girl."

Lady Jane Grey leapt forward, racing through the field. Paige's red hair tugged at her scalp as it streamed out behind her. Loud laughs and shouts pent-up for so long demanded to be released, so she laughed and yelled and cried all the way to the tree.

She couldn't decide if she would kill Uncle James for not telling her he'd sold her horse to the Halo M ranch or kiss him. It didn't matter. She and Lady Jane were back together, and for the first time in ten months, her world was tilting back into proper alignment.

Paige never looked behind her for Cash. Either he was with her or he wasn't. Whether getting him out of the house and onto a horse was a great idea or the worst one she'd ever had, she would soon know. As she neared the tree, she slowed. The sound of a horse galloping through the tall grass finally reached her hearing. With a quick glance, she saw Cash astride a large chestnut-brown horse. And surprise, surprise. A wide grin split his mouth, his white teeth clearly visible in the late-afternoon sun.

Reining Lady Jane to a stop, she allowed him to catch up. While she waited, she ran long strokes along Lady Jane Grey's neck. When Cash slowed and stopped next to her, he wore a smile she hadn't seen in years, one that went from his luscious lips to a devilish sparkle in his eyes. Without doubt, it was this expression that had so many women wanting Cash Montgomery in their beds. Not his fame, or his money, or even those huge silver prize buckles. It was the man himself.

"Looks like you haven't lost it," he said, reaching up to resettle his hat on his head.

"Thanks. I didn't realize how much I missed it." She leaned over and hugged the horse's neck. "And her."

"She's a beauty. What is she now? Sixteen?"

"More like twelve. She was five the last time I rode her and the gal's still got it." She continued stroking the horse. Lady Jane Grey looked wonderful. Healthy coat. Strong legs. Whatever Travis had been doing with her seemed to work.

"C'mon over the hill. There's a place where we can let the horses get a drink."

He turned to the left and cantered over the hill. Paige followed, still enjoying the fresh air and the feel of a strong, muscular horse between her legs. Lady Jane Grey followed Cash's gelding until Paige trotted up along aside.

"This is beautiful land. All Travis's?"

"Right now, we're passing onto my parents' land.

Their property and his butt together. Dad uses a lot of Travis's land for cattle grazing."

"Well, that's nice of Travis."

Cash chuckled. "Travis uses Dad's cattle to train his cutting horses, so it's a win-win for both of them."

They topped a hill and stopped. Below was a large lake. The afternoon sun sparkled on the water top. A breeze sent ripples rolling through the water.

"This view is breathtaking. How big is the lake?"

Cash shrugged. "It's a couple of acres, I think. It's fed by an underground spring, so even when we don't have much water, there will be some here. It's pretty deep too, so that helps keep a nice water level. Let's ride down."

They rode down the hillside, stopping at a hand pump with a spout over a large tub. Cash slid off his horse and led him to the tub. She tried not to notice his grimace when his left leg took his weight. He grabbed the handle and pumped water into the trough. Paige followed his lead, dropping from her horse and letting Lady Jane Grey drink.

"Why doesn't someone have a house here?" She turned in a full circle. "It's a perfect spot."

"There was one once. C'mon. I'll show you."

They tied off the horses and walked to another small hill. From the perspective, Paige could see the remains of a burned-out house, an old barn and a couple of outbuildings. Visually, that's what she saw, but mentally, she could picture an old house, chickens in the yard, kids running around the house. It was a pleasant vision.

"This was the original homestead. My great-great grandparents settled here. After they died and my great-grandfather married, he and Helen—that was my great-grandmother—lived here until the house burned. As nice as the area is, Helen was superstitious about rebuilding here. Plus, electricity was coming and she wanted to be closer to the road so they could get that new invention." He rolled his eyes, and they both laughed. "I know. I can't imagine no power. I mean, how could they charge their smartphones?"

"Smart ass," Paige said with a grin.

Cash slapped his rear. "Behave."

Paige just shook her head at his comedy routine, although she did have to admit, the man had a mighty nice butt. All those years of riding had made it firm and tight, and she'd love to get her hands on it one last time, not that that was going to happen.

"Anyway, Dad and Travis use the barns and outbuildings for storage." He backed toward the horses. "Ready?"

"Sure."

They got back to where they'd left the horses. Paige swung onto the back of Lady Jane Grey and watched Cash. The muscles in his jaw tightened when he put pressure on his left leg to lift his body into the saddle.

"Hurt?"

"What? Oh the leg? Nah."

Liar, liar. Pants on fire. But what would be the point in confronting him? So she let it drop.

"There's a loop around the lake. Ready?"

"Sure," she said. "Lead on."

They started out in a walk that quickly progressed to a fast trot. The constant movement of her horse as well as the off-and-on contact with her saddle had Paige's libido climbing. Being with the only man who'd truly held her heart might have been a contributing factor. She wasn't sure if she wanted to admit that or continue to pretend it was the riding.

They didn't talk as they rode. The silence could have been strained with anyone else, but today, in this setting, the quiet was relaxing.

She kept her eye on Cash, trying to ascertain if the riding was too much for his injuries. If not, he needed to be pushed to do as much as he was physically capable. Plus, having more to occupy his time might keep him away from the booze.

"By the way," she said, riding up next to him. "The back steps are awesome. Nice job."

"Thanks. All that wood was rotten. No telling how long it'd been there. Travis said to do whatever we wanted with the place and send him the bill." He looked at her with a totally evil grin. "I have plans."

She laughed. "Planning on bankrupting him?"

"Nope. But seriously, the exterior of the house needs painting and those steps were far from the only rotten wood I've seen."

"How do you know what to do? I mean, I wouldn't begin to know how to build stairs and stuff."

"Really? And you were doing so well with that hammer and nail."

She snorted.

"In the early years, when I wasn't cowboying somewhere, I worked construction crews. Good pay and the hard work kept me in condition. Back in the beginning, I didn't win enough to put gas in my truck to get me to the next rodeo. So I'd pick up jobs here and there."

"Oh. I forgot to ask. Did the plumber come today?"

"Yep, and everything's fine, except that back bedroom half-bath. It'll need a little work."

"So the plumber's coming back out then?"

"Bite your tongue. Of course not. I'll fix it."

She nodded, but inside her head, she grinned.

"I plan to paint the back steps and porch tomorrow, so don't use the back door."

She stopped her horse and waited until Cash stopped beside her. She leaned over, grabbed the front of his shirt and pulled him across for a kiss. The kiss was supposed to be a friendly, quick brush of her lips. It wasn't supposed to almost knock her off her horse, but Lord Almighty, the man still had the ability to melt her bones with a simple touch.

When she broke the kiss and pulled away, he shoved his hat up with a thumb and grinned. "What was that for?"

Turning Lady Jane Grey toward the barn, she smiled. "For fixing the back steps so I wouldn't trip." She urged her horse into a trot.

"Can't wait to see what you'll reward me with for a new whirlpool tub."

She flashed him a wicked grin. "I guess you'll have

to put one in and see." Then she charged away in a gallop.

When they got home, the aroma of roasting meat filled the house. Cash's stomach growled in anticipation.

"What can I do to help?" he asked, in a hurry to dig in.

"Wash up and then set the table, please. Oh, and let your dog out." Paige pulled the roast from the oven, the surrounding brown liquid bubbling around the potatoes and carrots. "I'll throw some biscuits in the oven while it's hot."

"He's not my dog," Cash protested as he headed for his bedroom. By the time Cash had the table set and Buster fed, Paige had sliced the roast and put bowls with the potatoes and carrots on the table. He grabbed the butter and jelly from the refrigerator, ready to slather the biscuits while they were hot.

"Milk, water, iced tea or Coke?" Paige asked, pulling two glasses from the cabinet.

Cash noticed the lack of alcoholic offerings. "Milk."

She nodded and poured two large glasses. She set those on the table then retrieved the platter of hot biscuits.

Dinner was pleasant. Conversation flowed easily between them. Cash found himself watching Paige's mouth as she ate or talked. Every time she dragged her fork between her full lips, he wanted to moan. When she darted her tongue out to lick a drop of milk off the corner of her mouth, his entire body noticed and hardened at the sight.

And no matter how many times he told himself that Paige was off-limits, that getting involved was the worst idea ever, his mind didn't want to pay attention It just kept producing erotic images…Paige naked in his bed, Paige's full lips wrapped around his hard penis, Paige holding her breasts up to his mouth…

"Cash. Are you listening to me?"

Cash startled. "Um, yes, I'm listening. You were talking about some patient you saw today, right?"

Paige rolled her eyes. "Yeah, about ten minutes ago. I was asking if you'd mind cleaning up the kitchen. I'd like to take a shower and go to bed early to do a little reading."

"Oh, sure. No problem."

"Thanks." She slid her chair back and stood. After scraping her plate into the trash, she set the dirty dish, utensils and drinking glass in the sink. "The plastic wrap to cover the food is in this drawer," she said with a tilt of her head to the right. "I'll see you in the morning. Thanks." She headed out of the kitchen with a wave of her hand.

Cash stared at the leftover food and sighed. Standing, he began gathering up the dishes. After storing the food in the refrigerator and washing the dishes they'd used, he and Buster went outside for an evening walk. But he couldn't get the image of Paige in the shower out of his mind's eye or escape the erotic suggestions his mind was making.

The walk outside cleared his head enough that he

was sure he could sleep. He headed back to his lumpy bed and tried to find a position that was at least tolerable. One more night with the crappy bed and then he'd be sleeping on a cloud. If only he had a drink or two to help ease him to sleep.

He tossed and turned until sometime after midnight when Buster woke him with a cold nose and a whimper. Afterwards, he decided Buster had the right idea. With the half-bath out of commission until he had time to repair it, he headed to Paige's bathroom. Done answering nature's call, he was headed back to his room when he heard a cry. He stepped over to Paige's closed door and listened. It wasn't long before he heard her sob.

He opened her door. "Paige?" he whispered. "Are you okay?"

"Mom. Dad." Paige's sobs grew louder. "No. Stop. Don't die. Mom. Dad." She thrashed around in her bed, tossing her bedcovers off. "Somebody help them. Help. Cash. Oh my God. Cash."

Cash hurried to her bedside. "Paige. Wake up. You're dreaming." He touched her gently on the shoulder. "Wake up."

She cried out again and then jerked to a sitting position. "What? Cash?" She wiped her face on her T-shirt sleeve. "Oh, I was dreaming."

"Scoot over," he said, hip bumping her. When she didn't move, he bumped her again. "Scoot."

She shifted to the right side of the bed and Cash slipped onto the left side. After pulling her sheet back up, he put his arm around her.

"Want to tell me about your dream?"

For a minute, she was rigid, and then her muscles relaxed and she sagged against him.

"It's all jumbled. First it was their accident…Mom and Dad's." A shudder wracked her body. "It was horrible. The loud crash. The screeching of the metal." Tears trickled down her cheeks. Cash wiped her tears with his thumb.

"I didn't know you were there."

"I was in my car behind them because they were going on up to Northern California and I was planning on heading home." She drew in a ragged breath. "It was horrible."

He pulled her tight against him and stroked her hair. "I can't imagine."

"And then…" She hiccupped a sob. "And then I saw you get stomped by that damn bull. Everybody I loved was dying right in front of my eyes."

His gut clenched at the mention of love. "Shh." He pressed her head to his chest. "I'm fine. Nobody dying here."

"I…" Her breaths came in shuddered waves.

"Don't cry," he said. "Here, scoot down and rest. You have a busy day tomorrow."

He pulled her lower in the bed as he slid down. Once he got settled, she put her head on his chest. He wondered if she could hear his heart racing. She'd scared at least two years off his life when she'd cried out. She'd been so much pain when her parents died and then she'd watched his own brush with death thanks to Bad Bob. He hated that sharing this house might produce such emotionally draining nightmares for her. Somehow, he would find a way to make up for all the crap he'd dumped in her life.

"God, your mattress is as bad as mine." He shifted in an attempt to move his ass off a particularly hard lump. "Maybe worse."

She snorted. "I know. Isn't it awful?" She released a wistful sigh. "I miss the gel-filled foam mattress I was sleeping on at Uncle James's house. It was like floating on a cloud."

He made a note to call the furniture store first thing tomorrow morning. He may have been a total ass in her past, but maybe he could atone a little now with a decent mattress. It was the least he could do.

"Okay then…" he wiggled his hips, "…I've got the worst lump flattened. You need to sleep."

She yawned. "I'm okay now. You don't have to stay." But even as she said the words, her head grew heavier on his chest as she relaxed.

He didn't reply. Instead, he continued to stroke her hair and rub her back until her breathing became slow and regular.

Bright moonlight streamed through the window, giving him enough light to see that her eyes were shut, her light lashes resting on her round cheeks.

"Are you asleep?" he whispered. When she gave no response, he said, "I wish things could have been different with us. If I could go back and change the past, I would never have walked away from you. I really cared for you…maybe too much. But it's too late now. You deserve so much more than a broken-down cowboy with a questionable future."

She shifted, scooting closer and nuzzling her head under his chin. Her soft flesh pressed into his side. He froze, wondering if she'd heard him. But a light snore from her reassured him his secret was safe.

He thought that he might still be in love her, but nothing would happen between them. He wouldn't pursue a future with her. It wouldn't be a good life for her.

"You're safe with me. I won't make it hard on either of us. I promise not to kiss you again or try to get you in bed. I'll be your best friend." He sealed his promise with a press of his lips on the top of her head. The scent of fresh lilacs filled his senses. He drew in a deep breath and let the sweet aroma set a memory in his mind.

So Cash believed she was safe with him. He believed he got to define their relationship, did he? Didn't she have any say at all? What an idiot. She couldn't believe he fell for that fake snore.

Dumb-ass.

Goose bumps popped on her arms as she thought about how gently he'd stroked her hair. When he'd left that kiss on her head, it was all she could do not to turn in his arms and rip his inane restraint to shreds.

Hmm. Maybe that's what she should do. Hook him like a fish, reel him in and then brutally cut line like he had her.

But he'd felt so good next to her last night. Even with the rock-hard lump under her hip, she hadn't moved away. When she'd awoken this morning still wrapped in his arms, it had taken every ounce of willpower to slide from the bed. Shockingly, he hadn't moved.

She'd left him cinnamon rolls and a fresh pot of coffee for breakfast. Wonder what he thought about that? Did he smile when he saw them? Would he have licked the icing off his fingers? Licked his lips? Think about her as he ate them? Wonder—

"Paige?"

Paige jumped at the sound of her name. "What?"

Dr. Lydia Henson smiled at her. "You were a million miles away."

"Just thinking. Sorry. Here's the file on your next patient." She passed the medical chart to Lydia, who nodded when she saw the name on the tab.

"Ah, yes. Mr. Francis. We all know him well. Come on. Time you meet our favorite patient."

The day rolled by slowly. Paige didn't want to admit how badly she wanted to go home. The nursing work was fine and the clinic staff had all been friendly and helpful, but she couldn't get the damn man at home out of her head.

She pulled her car around to the back of the house ready to climb the back steps. It wasn't until she saw the rope tied across the bottom step that she remembered Cash had said he was planning on painting today, and he had. Brilliant, almost blinding white paint covered the new stairs, handrail and back porch.

He'd even found time to paint the back door a glossy green. She restarted her car and pulled to the front of the house.

"Hey! You here?" she called, walking in the front door.

"Upstairs. Come up and tell me what you think."

Paige climbed the stairs, picking up Ruby from the middle step and carrying her along. The change was dramatic enough to have her gasping with surprised pleasure. "Wow. You have a great eye for decorating."

The upstairs open area now sported a purple, turquoise and brown geometric design rug. The furniture—a set of cushy recliners and a full-sized sofa—were a rich mahogany leather. Light-colored wood and glass end tables flanked the sofa and filled the area between the chairs. "This is beautiful." A huge—eighty-inch was her guess—flat-screen television completed the room.

"And in here, no more lumpy bed." He swept his arm toward the large bedroom at the front of the house.

Inside was a king-sized bed with a leather headboard and bedside tables with marble inlays, plus a matching dresser.

"Nice," she said with a nod. "Very nice."

Buster bounded out of the bedroom to greet her. "Hey, Buster." She sat Ruby on the floor and the two pets started a game of tag up and down the stairs.

"Glad you approve. There was an armoire I wanted but I didn't think it would fit in the room." He looked around. "Now that it's all in here, I know it wouldn't."

"Well, color me jealous," she said with a laugh.

"Aww," he said, wrapping an arm around her shoulders. "I'll let you rent my room whenever you want."

She punched his side with her elbow. "Meany." She slipped from under his arm. "By the way, the back porch looks great." She headed for the stairs and then looked over her shoulder. "How's your leg holding up with all the physical labor?"

He rubbed his thigh. "A little achy but I'll live."

"I'm going to change before dinner. Leftover roast."

"Sounds great."

She went to her room, unbuttoning her blouse as soon as she got to the hallway. Her bedroom door was open, which was odd because she was sure she'd closed it this morning. She let out an ear-splitting scream when she looked in.

"Andrew Lane Montgomery. I can't believe you did this," she yelled and then flopped in the middle of her new gel-filled foam mattress. "Oh my God. This is wonderful." She rolled from side-to-side, giggling with glee. "I can't believe it."

"One night was all it took for me. I don't know how you've slept there a week."

She leaned up on her elbows. "Thank you. I can't believe it. I just can't. You didn't have to do this."

He gave her one of his lecherous grins. "Nice look."

Paige looked down and got a great view of her beige bra through the unbuttoned front of her shirt. "Oh crap." She jerked the sides together.

"I've seen a bra before, Paige. Chill."

She snorted. Of course he had. Plenty of them was her guess. Nonetheless, what he'd done for her, replacing her god-awful bag of rocks disguised as a mattress, deserved at least a kiss.

The grin on his face faltered a little as she neared. "Thank you, Cash. I'll pay you back. I swear. Every penny." She arched up on her toes, held his face in her hands and pulled him lower for a kiss. It started as a press of lips. Simple. Sweet. Innocent. Then she felt the palm of his large hand at the base of her neck sliding into her hair. He pulled back until their gazes met.

"You don't owe me anything. Certainly not for this mattress."

He took her mouth in a hard kiss that quickly became greedy and demanding. The tip of his tongue tickled at her lips. When she parted them, he thrust into her mouth, his tongue filling the cavity, touching and stroking every centimeter. She moved her tongue against his. Electrified at his taste, buzzed by the sheer pleasure at his mastery of a simple kiss, she put all she had into the kiss.

Her nervous system flipped into overdrive. Heart palpitations. Choppy breathing, when she could draw a breath. Toes curled under. Hells bells. She was sweating behind her knees.

When he spread his other hand across her shoulders and he pulled her tight against him, his hard shaft pressed into her stomach. She squeezed her eyes shut. It was too much. He was too much. She wanted more. She wanted everything.

Instead, she pushed away on unsteady legs.

"This isn't a good idea," she managed to squeak out. Her voice was raspy, raw, as affected by the kiss as the rest of her. "We have to live together. Get along for the next few months. I—"

"No, you're right." He backed up. "Sorry. I—"

"No, it's was my fault." She took a couple of steps away. "I'll just finish changing clothes and get started on dinner."

"I just remembered I'm supposed to be somewhere." He turned and headed back into the hall. "I'll be back later. Don't hold dinner for me. I'll grab something while I'm out."

"Wait, Cash. You don't have to leave."

"Yeah, I do."

He turned and, walking with long strides, was gone. She heard the front door slam, his truck fire up, and rocks crunching as he tore down the drive. Sitting on the side of her bed, she drew in a deep breath. Well, hell.

She kept expecting him home all evening, but when he hadn't returned by eleven, she took Buster outside for his nightly walk, killing a little more time. Finally, she had to get to bed if she wanted to have a functioning brain in the morning. Taking Buster and Ruby with her, she sank into her new bed and slept the sleep of the dead.

CASH SAT IN THE DRIVE STARING AT OLD MAN Fitzgerald's house. What had he been thinking? He lifted the bourbon bottle to his mouth, took a long swig and then wiped his mouth with the back of his hand. Paige Ryan deserved a man who could give her kids, a stable future. He wasn't that man.

He took another gulp of the booze, feeling the satisfying burn as it slid down his throat. His brothers were right. He didn't deserve a woman like Paige, not that they'd ever said those words, but it'd been obvious at dinner on Sunday. When Caroline suggested matchmaking Paige with the new sheriff's department deputy, there'd been a general consensus around the table of the brilliance of that idea because, after all, Marc Singer might make excellent husband material. Not one person had suggested Cash might be a good catch.

He poured the rest of the bottle of bourbon in his mouth. Nope. He wiped his hand across his lips. Nobody had given little brother a second of thought. Not one member of his family saw him as anything other than a loser. General consensus there too. Hell, he agreed with them.

He climbed from his truck and stumbled over the rocky drive to the house. He should just move out, but he wasn't going to. He liked the little area he'd set up.

The front door was unlocked. After letting himself in, he locked it and stumbled up the stairs. He stepped on something and jumped when it squeaked. Oh crap. Buster. He'd forgotten about Buster.

"Buster," he called in a hushed tone. "Where are you, boy? Come here." He clapped his hands but the dog didn't come. In the quiet house, he thought he heard a bark. Following the quiet yips, he traced Buster to Paige's bedroom. He opened the door far enough for the dog to get out but not so far that he'd be able to see Paige. If she was awake, he didn't want to see the censure in her eyes. If she was asleep, he was afraid he'd stay watching her like some pervert. Instead, he collected the dog that wasn't his from the bedroom of the woman who could never be his and headed to his own bed.

Chapter Seven

The next couple of weeks, Paige and Cash maintained a polite distance. For breakfast, Paige would gulp down a cup of coffee while chewing on a breakfast bar. Then she'd rush out of the house for work. Cash would have a couple of cups of coffee while he scanned the newspaper. Of course they'd say good morning, and at bedtime, good night, but in between, the conversation was as impersonal as two strangers sharing adjoining seats on a plane.

Cash continued to work on the exterior of the house, finding more boards that time and weather had eaten away. When he began painting the exterior, the wood sucked up the paint like water poured on sand. The sun-exposed side required three coats of white while the others seemed to be satisfied after two.

The first week of hard labor had left him sore and stiff, his leg letting him know every night how displeased it was. However, by the end of the second week, his pain was manageable with a couple of aspirin. After his shower every evening, he was too tired to do much more than eat whatever Paige put on the table and then crash upstairs in front of his television.

Three weeks after their devastating kiss, Cash was tired of staying home and tired of Paige's guarded facade around him. He put up his tools early and took his shower, ready to suggest dinner out when Paige returned. Besides, it was the Friday night of Memorial Day weekend. She'd been doing all the cooking, mostly because his cooking wasn't edible. She deserved a nice night out. Plus, dinner out with Paige was the perfect way to start a long holiday weekend.

At close to five, he heard her car pull up the drive. He met her at the front door with his friendliest smile, the one that always won the ladies.

"Hey. How about dinner at the Longstar Grill? Or we can go to that new Italian place if you want. I owe you about dozen meals."

His heart skittered when she smiled. "That's sounds wonderful, Cash, but I already have plans for tonight."

His smile faltered. "You do? Dinner plans?"

"I'm sorry. If I'd known, I'd have told Marc no."

"Marc?"

"Marc Singer. A deputy with the sheriff's department. Lydia introduced us. Anyway, we've had lunch a couple of times, and when he dropped by today, he asked if I wanted to try Amore's, which is so strange since I was telling you the other night about it. So I said yes." She checked her watch. "I need to get moving if I want to get a shower and freshen up before he gets here." She took a couple of steps and then turned back to him. "Do you want me to put something on for dinner for you before I leave?"

"No. Don't worry about me." He tried for a flippant, disaffected tone, not sure if he achieved it or not. "Great about your date. We'll do dinner out another time."

"Well." She drew the word out. "If you're sure." She took another couple of steps and stopped. "Are you sure you don't mind if I go out?"

Of course he minded. The oh-so-perfect deputy. Didn't anyone in his blasted family realize that Paige deserved more than a guy who might get shot down on the job? Besides, every redneck deputy Cash knew was at least fifty pounds overweight and had the personality of jackasses, braying and bragging about everything. And now that he thought about it, Caroline hadn't said anything about the guy being attractive, only that he was nice.

Ha! Nice! The kiss of death for a guy.

"Of course I don't mind," he said with a straight face. "Why would I care if my roomie has a date? You have fun."

She shrugged. "Okay." She rounded the corner and headed down the short hall to her room.

Cash dropped onto the steps and Buster bounded up to him as though saying, "Yay. Let's play," and dropped a tennis ball beside Cash's feet. He lobbed the ball through the living room and into the dining room. The puppy, his paws too big for his body, flung himself off the step after the ball, his uncoordinated lope bringing a grin to Cash's face.

When was the last time he'd tried to find a home for Buster? The gangly puppy trotted back to him with the bright-yellow ball clutched in his mouth.

"Drop it."

Buster released the ball immediately. He might be a little clumsy and his ears long enough to drag the floor, but Buster was smart. He learned commands after only a couple of tries. No matter how long Cash left Buster outside, the dog never wandered off. It was as if he'd decided he'd found his home. And now that he'd spent some time thinking about it, it'd been at least a couple of weeks since he'd offered Buster to someone, and even that offer had been half-hearted at best.

He and Buster headed back upstairs. The last thing he wanted to see was Paige all made up for another guy, even if he was probably fifty pounds overweight. He dropped into a leather recliner and turned on the local news.

The craving for a beer haunted him in the worst way. It'd been weeks since he'd had a drink, and what had that gotten him? Paige hadn't noticed. His family probably still considered him a drunk and a total loser. Olivia and Mitch's opinions of him couldn't get much lower. They'd even given up on inviting him over for dinner,

The rumble of a diesel truck in the drive had him

pushing down the footrest and heading for the stairs. He might not want to see Paige, but he did want to get an eye on the guy picking her up. He'd make sure this deputy understood that Paige was special and he'd better treat her right.

Cash flung open the front door after a single knock, hoping Marc Singer was fat and balding with rotten teeth and bad breath. Fuck. He was as tall as Cash with black hair cut very short. When he smiled, his teeth damn near blinded Cash. What was this guy? A toothpaste model on the side?

"Hi." Marc shoved his hand forward. "I'm Marc Singer. You must be Cash Montgomery."

Cash took his hand in a bruising grip. "I am." He didn't try to make his voice less brusque. "Paige tells me you are talking her to Amore's. That's nice. What time will you be back?"

"Okay, Dad. Stop it." Paige came up behind him with a laugh. "Mom said I could stay out until midnight now that I'm twenty-one."

Marc chuckled.

Paige stepped around Cash. "Hi, Marc. I guess you've met my guard dog, Cash."

Marc nodded. "I did. I've heard so much about him from Lydia that I feel like I already know him." He looked at Cash. "Quite an impressive career. Don't know how you got on the backs of those crazy bulls. I know I could never do it."

Now Cash was getting really mad. Not only was the man obviously attractive, he was nice. And his breath was minty fresh when he spoke.

Damn it.

"You just get on and hang on," Cash replied. "Just takes some balls. You have some balls, right?"

"Well, we'd better go," Paige said, effectively putting a stop to Cash's testosterone-induced posturing.

"You're right," Marc said. "Nice to meet you, Cash." He stepped back to allow Paige through the door.

"Don't wait up," she whispered to Cash.

Fuck.

He was at a loss of how to spend his evening now that his original plan had just left in a shiny black truck. Absentmindedly, he tossed the tennis ball from hand to hand as he debated his options. He could go to Leo's, but Leo was such an old woman these days. He'd be on the phone to Cash's brothers before Cash could get half a beer down. There was that other hole-in-the-wall joint, Maxine's. But sitting and drinking all evening didn't hold much appeal these days.

Buster barked and Cash realized the poor dog had been watching the tennis ball for the past few minutes, just waiting for Cash to play.

"Sorry, boy." Cash arced the ball toward the dining room and the puppy tore out. Balls. He'd told the deputy that riding a bull took balls, and it did. Somewhere, Cash's balls had shriveled up with his nerve. He needed to go to see Olivia and Mitch. Hell, he needed to talk to Mitch about his investment, and yet he didn't have enough balls to drive onto their property. Fuck that.

He pulled his phone from his pocket and scrolled through the directory until he found the number for Kickin' Bull Ranch. His sister answered.

"Hey, sis. What's going on out there? I thought maybe I could take you up on one of your dinner invitations."

"Sorry, little bro. My darling husband is taking me to Amore's for dinner. That's that new Italian place."

"Yes. I'm aware."

"I've been waiting to go since its opening a couple of weeks ago. Took this long for us to get reservations, so as much as I'd love to have you out, afraid it'll have to be another night."

Amore's? What the….? Was the place giving away meals tonight?

"No problem. I just found my evening free and I've been promising to come out so I thought maybe our nights might match up. No big deal. Ask Mitch if we can get together about the business next week"

"I'm sure he can, but I'll let him know to call you."

"Have a nice meal."

Wasn't his night getting better and better? He considered calling his parents, but the thought of his mother's sincere but smothering love was more than he could take this evening.

Travis and Caroline had only been home for a month with the twins, so he didn't imagine they'd be interested in him dropping by. He called Jason's cell phone. The background noise when his brother answered suggested he was in a car.

"Hey," Cash said. "What's going on?"

"Not much. Lydia and I are headed out for dinner."

"Any place good?"

"Amore's. We're meeting some people there."

"Oh. Well, I'll let you go."

"No, that's okay. What'd you need?"

"Nothing." He paused. "Mitch and Olivia are headed there. So are Paige and Marc Singer."

The pregnant pause on his brother's end was deafening. "Yeah. I know."

"So you all meeting there for dinner?"

Jason cleared his throat. "Yeah."

"Travis and Caroline too?"

"Well…it's just that…" He cleared his throat again. "It's just that Lydia thought it might be nice if all of us got together."

"Us?"

"You know. A couples sort of thing."

"So Paige and this guy are a couple?"

"I don't know, Cash. I just go where Lydia tells me. Listen, I need to run. We're at the restaurant. I'll give you a shout tomorrow, okay? Glad you called. Let's get together soon."

During his phone calls, Cash had paced from the living room, into the dining room, out the side door in the dining room and onto the trellis-covered deck at the side of the house. After Jason clicked off, Cash stood holding his phone not quite sure what he was feeling inside. Frustrated? Yep. Mad? Yep. Confused that his brothers and sister hadn't included him in the dinner plans? Most definitely.

He *got* that this was a couples thing, but he could have found a date if they'd given him advance notice. If his sister-in-law hadn't been such an activist in matching his roommate up with the new deputy, he could have brought Paige. She'd fit nicely with his family.

Shit. She *was* fitting nicely into his family. He was the one on the outside. Hell of a thing when an outsider meshed better with his family than he did.

After a dinner of peanut butter and jelly sandwiches, he went upstairs to find something on television to watch. Even Ruby and Butch had deserted him to play tag with each other.

He was a single shoe in a closet of pairs.

He popped the back of his recliner into sitting when the slam of a truck door echoed in the quiet night. Rolling his gaze to the left, he saw that it was late, almost midnight. That was a long damn dinner. Whispering Springs was a small community, certainly not large enough to support much night life other than bars. Granted, there were nights when Leo's had live music, but since he hadn't been there in over a month, he had no idea if that's where they might have been. Plus, he couldn't imagine Olivia and Caroline staying away from the children until midnight.

How should he play this? Stay up here? Let the cop get his goodnight kiss at the door? Oh crap. What if she brought him back to her bed? He didn't think he could take that. He might have to kill the bastard.

He bided his time, listening for the front door to open. If the sonofabitch came in with her, he could make the situation uncomfortable enough that maybe he'd leave.

The squeak in the hinge of the front door—the one he'd been meaning to oil—alerted him that someone was entering. Maybe oiling that squeak could wait a while longer.

As much as he didn't want to, as much as he hated he couldn't control his actions, he looked over the railing into the living room. Paige was alone. She was bending over to pet Buster and Ruby, giving him an excellent view of her ass.

"Have fun?"

She startled and looked up. A smile slowly crawled across her mouth. "I did. The food was wonderful."

Her cherry-red lipstick was slightly smeared off her upper lip on the right side. An unwanted ping of jealousy rattled his gut.

He gritted his teeth, but the question got out anyway. "Does he kiss good?"

Her eyes opened wide in surprise.

"Come on up. I'd love to hear all about it." His knuckles were white where he'd wrapped his fingers around the railing.

"It's late." She looked away and stood. "I should get some—"

"If you won't come up, I'll come down."

She made the mistake of looking up toward Cash

again. He wasn't at the railing. Her heart leapt at the vision of him hurrying down the stairs. Dressed in a pair of sweat pants that'd been cut off at the knees and a torn work-out shirt, he appeared bigger than life, tougher than beef jerky. His bare feet slapped on the polished wood of each step. She suddenly had a flashback to the night of her eighteenth birthday. The warrior charging across a battlefield. She needed to move, to run to her bedroom and slam the door, but she couldn't. Her feet were glued to the floor. A battle of mind versus heart. Tonight, her heart was stronger.

He stopped in front of her. His body heat didn't. It swept forward, wrapped around her, swaddled her in warmth. Pulled by all that power and energy, she swayed. He caught her face between the palms of his hands, wrapping his fingers around her head and into her hair.

"Did he kiss you like this?" he said in a breathy whisper against her lips. And then he took her mouth in a savage kiss. All lips and teeth, touching, grinding, nibbling.

She parted her lips, welcomed his tongue inside, greeted him with a long, hard suck on his tongue. The room swam and she leaned into him for stability. Her entire world shrank down to him, his mouth, his tongue. Filling her. Making her feel alive. Desirable. No longer alone.

He jerked his mouth away, trailed kisses along her jaw and up to her ear. The steamy breath from his lips trickled into her ear, igniting a firestorm of lust in her gut. Her knees softened. She grabbed his waist to hold her upright.

At least, that's what she meant to do. Instead, when her fingers touched the hot flesh peeking between his T-shirt and shorts, she couldn't stop herself from pulling him snuggly against her.

He attacked her mouth again with a deep, wet kiss. A deep-throated groan echoed in the room amid the sounds of wet kisses and moans. Her groan? His? She didn't know. What she did know was he was as affected by her as she by him, as evidenced by the long, hard cock pressed into her stomach. She kicked off her shoe and ran her heel up his bare leg to his thigh, his rough leg hair scraping the bottom of her foot. Then she wrapped her leg around his until she could press her throbbing sex against his thigh.

Gliding his hand down her neck, he trailed his fingers to the swell of her breasts. He used the tips of his fingers to tease her flesh at the vee of her buttoned blouse.

Her breath became erratic, choppy and short. Her insides liquefied and flowed to her core, making her panties wet with desire. She slid her hands under his shirt, felt the ridges of muscles, traced the ribs up until she met his crinkly chest hair. Then she felt the tough skin of multiple scars.

He stilled and pulled away. "I'm sorry. I shouldn't have done that." Stepping back, his gaze froze on her face. "I…" He turned away and started for the stairs.

"Wait. Cash. I don't understand. Why did you stop?"

He shook his head and continued up the stairs. She heard his bedroom door slam.

Sexually frustrated, overly exhausted and too tense to sleep, Paige went to the kitchen and spent the next two hours baking cookies. Finally, at close to three in the morning, she shut herself away in her bedroom and dropped into a restless sleep.

Blinding rays of bright sun streaming through her window gave Paige an abrupt and rude wakening. Rolling away, she shielded her eyes with the extra pillow on her bed. She lay there listening to the air conditioner drone on until it shut off. The sudden quiet sharpened her hearing for any movement in the house. Was Cash still here? What would he say about last night? What would she say? She didn't know. Heck, she didn't know what she felt or how she should feel.

She groaned and pulled the pillow tight over her head. Why couldn't life be simpler? Why couldn't she have fallen madly in lust with Marc last night?

It wasn't easy, but she pulled herself far enough out of her funk to get dressed. She found a note on the kitchen table that said nothing beyond *Be back late*. After wadding it into a tight ball, she shot it for a three-pointer at the trash can. Of course she missed and didn't that just about sum up her life.

From the other end of the house, her cell phone trilled. She hurried back to her bedroom to where she'd left her phone charging.

"Hello?"

"Good morning, Paige. It's Marc."

Paige sat on the edge of her bed. "Good morning, Marc." She wasn't disappointed that it was him, but she found that her heart didn't race at the sound of his voice. He was a nice guy. Considerate. Handsome. Smart. She could do worse.

And at that thought, her eyes rolled toward the ceiling. Much worse.

"I hope you slept well."

"Like a baby." If the baby was a newborn with colic.

"I wondered if you had plans for today. I know it's short notice, but an old friend and his wife are having a last-minute Memorial Day cookout this afternoon, then going to watch the fireworks downtown. I told him I'd come. I'd love if you'd go with me."

"This afternoon?"

"I know. Short notice. I'm sorry about that. But I had such a nice time last night. I wasn't ready for it to be over. Say you'll come."

"I…" What did she have on her schedule today? Running the vacuum was about it. Let's see…running a vacuum or a date with a good-looking, nice guy? Is that even a contest? "I'd love to. What time?"

"I'll pick you up about three. Does that work?"

"Sure. See you then."

She had to get on with life. Other than a couple of kisses—damn hot kisses, but still just kisses—Cash had pretty much let her know he obviously found her attractive, but he didn't have a need for her in his life. The sooner she could convince herself of that fact, the sooner she could move on and find someone to start a life with. It might not be Marc Singer, but at least she was doing something, getting out there, meeting people. No telling where that could lead.

CASH WAVED THE WAITRESS OVER FOR A COFFEE refill. As soon as she left, he looked at Mitch Landry. "So I guess you're wondering why you're here this morning."

Mitch yawned. "Not really. Olivia said you wanted to discuss our business. You ready to get your hands dirty?"

"That's just the thing. I'm not."

Mitch set his coffee down and frowned. "I don't get it. What do you mean you're not?"

Cash fiddled with the handle of his coffee, trying to find the right words until he realized there were no right words, only blunt ones. "I don't want to be in the bull business. Not anymore."

"I see. This was your idea. Remember?"

Cash shrugged. "Sure, but let's face it. My life hasn't exactly gone according to plans over the past eight months or so."

"So what? You want me to buy you out?" Mitch shook his head. "I'm cash short. Everything I've got is tied up in land and cattle. You want to tell me why you've changed your mind?"

In Cash's mind, the baby Brahma bull sneered. "I just don't want anything to do with bull riding, at least not right now." He crossed his arms on the table and leaned forward. "I don't want you to buy me out. I want to stay your partner, or at least your investor. You're a hell of a cattleman and an even better businessman." He leaned back in the booth. "I've just lost my interest in the cattle ranching business."

The men sat quietly in the booth at the Chew Shop. Cash took a bite of his everything-but-the-kitchen-sink omelet and waited. How the hell could he tell his brother-in-law that the thought of being around bulls made his balls pull up into his abdomen?

Finally, Mitch nodded. "Is this why you won't come to our house for dinner? I don't know how many times your sister has asked you. You weren't ready to discuss this yet?"

"Something like that."

Mitch leaned forward, his voice pitched so low Cash could barely hear him. "Let me make something clear, Cash. My wife loves you. I love my wife. I'll do whatever it takes to make her happy. If dragging your ass to our house for dinner is necessary, I'll do that. I'd rather not. I'd rather you tell me the truth on why you're avoiding Olivia." Cash could see the muscles in his brother-in-law's face tighten and he suspected Mitch was gritting his teeth in anger.

"Fine," Cash said, his tone resigned. "It has nothing to do with Olivia. Or you, for that matter. I…" He glanced nervously around the room then leaned closer to Mitch. "You're gonna think I'm crazy. It's the fucking bulls. I…I can't stand to be around them. There. Are you satisfied?" He drew back and crossed his arms. "Are you happy now? You know my big secret. I can't stand being around the fucking bulls."

Puzzlement followed by understanding flashed on Mitch's face. "I don't know why I didn't see this. It makes total sense. Of course it makes sense. Hell, Cash. You should have said something sooner."

Cash rubbed his forehead, doing nothing for the headache that was starting. "Really?" he asked in a sarcastic tone. "You think I want everybody to know that Cash Montgomery is afraid of bulls. Oh hell, yeah. That'll be great for my reputation."

Mitch nodded. "Got it."

"So this conversation remains between us?"

"It's a business meeting. Of course it's confidential."

"Thanks, man."

"So back to Kickin' Bull Ranch."

"You still want to pursue raising bulls for the PBR or were you just doing this for Olivia's little brother?"

Mitch grinned. "A little of both probably. But without your influence, I'm not sure I have a solid plan."

The two men spent the next two hours talking about the business, contractors for the PBR, the realities of raising the bulls and getting them on the rodeo circuit. At the end, it was decided that raising bulls was more Cash's dream than Mitch's. Mitch loved the land, loved raising the cattle. Without Cash as his business partner, Mitch confessed his heart wasn't in raising rodeo bulls. Since most of Mitch's liquid assets were tied up, and Cash didn't really need his investment in Kickin' Bull Ranch, the men agreed that Cash would remain as a minority partner. Seemed like a win-win for both of them.

"So now what?" Mitch asked as they walked out to their trucks.

"Don't know. I'm enjoying rehabbing the Fitzgerald place for now. I've got a lot more to do. When that's done, who knows? Maybe I'll find another place that needs to be renovated." He shrugged. "For now, I'm just taking it a day at a time."

"You will come to dinner? Soon? Olivia misses you."

"I'll come," Cash said with a smile. He held out his hand. "Thanks, Mitch."

"No problem, man. See you soon."

Cash waited until Mitch had driven off to start his engine. He didn't want to go home, not yet. He'd replaced all the rotten wood. Rebuilt the front porch railing. Finished painting the exterior with a bright white. He decided to do the front door in a red. Somewhere he remembered red being a lucky color for a front door, and God knew he needed all the luck he could get.

The plan for this week focused on cleaning the patio area just off the dining room, which involved a lot of power washing of the brickwork and the wrought-iron furniture there. Years of neglect and rain had left the wrought iron corroded with rust. The furniture was in severe need of sanding to remove the oxide followed by rust-protective paint. But he wasn't in the mood to do that.

He was in the mood to drink, to get rip-roaring drunk. So drunk that he wouldn't see Paige's face everywhere. Wouldn't see her smile. Hear her laugh. Taste her in his mouth. He needed a fifth of Jack Daniels.

Instead, he called his brother.

"Hey, Travis."

"Cash. Missed you at dinner last night."

"Yeah, well. Listen, you still okay with me putting some of your money into the Singing Springs house?"

His brother chuckled. "Now what?"

"I've been needing to redo the small half-bath in the back bedroom, and with three more bedrooms upstairs, this room hasn't been needed. But I thought maybe I'd make the half-bath into a full bath. Something nice. And then maybe add a hot tub outside the patio area off the dining room."

"Uh-huh. What is this going to cost me?"

"Tell you what. I'll run some figures by your place this afternoon. If it's too much, I'll just do what has to be done to repair that tiny, old, out-of-date bathroom."

Travis laughed. "Come on by. Make it close to lunch."

"Great. See you then."

THE LUNCH VISIT WITH TRAVIS AND CAROLINE evolved into a ride on horseback over to Singing Springs to show Travis the work Cash had already finished.

"This looks great, Cash. Seriously." Travis walked around the exterior of the house. "I thought the house probably had good bones, but you've done an excellent job bringing her back to her old self." He looked at Cash. "I bet even old grumpy Angus Fitzgerald would have to approve."

Cash laughed. "You think? That's high praise."

"So show me again what you're wanting to do."

Cash led him around to the side of the house where the patio off the dining room was located. "I found this while I was working." He indicated an almost-hidden metal door. "It was completely overgrown with poison ivy. It wasn't until I killed the ivy back that I saw it. The hinges were rusty and the door was hell to get open, but look." Cash turned the handle and pulled up on the door. "Hold on. Let me grab a flashlight. Can't see a thing without it."

Cash made a quick dash into the house for a light, surprised to find the place empty except for Ruby and Buster. Paige hadn't said anything about plans today, but then again, he hadn't seen her since last night's lapse of judgment.

He returned with a powerful six-battery flashlight and shined it down into the opening.

"What is it?" Travis asked.

"Tornado shelter, I think. Looks like it probably began as some type of basement or root cellar. Over time, Fitzgerald had it remade into a storm shelter. Did you know it was here?"

Travis shook his head. "I had no idea. You been down?"

"Yeah, and it's pretty cool. Needs to be cleaned up, but I can't imagine anywhere safer in a tornado. I don't think anyone's been down there in years though. Want to go look?"

Travis gave him a look of incredulity. "You're kidding, right? Of course I'm going in to look around."

Cash secured the hatch with a rope tied to the patio trellis. "I didn't want it to shut behind us."

"Good thinking."

The underground bunker was a small twelve-by-twelve-foot room with concrete walls and floor. It was furnished with two folding chairs, a card table and a kerosene lamp. Two bunk-style beds were suspended from one wall.

"I'm surprised it's not mustier smelling," Travis said as he looked around.

"It was. I've had the door open for the past week airing it out."

"So what are you wanting to do?"

"I'd like to run some electricity down here for some lights. I'm not sure about air circulation, but I'd like to get someone out here who knows more about storm shelters to look it over and advise me—us—on how to modernize it and make sure it's up to code. No reason to have something like this and not have it usable."

"I totally agree, and I have to admit, it's not something I've ever thought about. But with Caroline and the two babies, well, maybe I should. Let's go back up top."

Cash followed Travis up the steep ladder back outside.

"Do some research, would you? Find out who's the best company in this area." Travis looked around. "I assume you're going to clear out the path to get here easier."

"Yup. Just hadn't gotten to it yet. Come over here." Cash walked off toward the patio, Travis following. "What would you think about me installing a hot tub out here? I'd probably extend the decking so to not lose any square footage from this patio area, but the privacy is perfect."

Travis arched an eyebrow. "Privacy? A hot tub? Just exactly what's going on over here?"

Cash slugged Travis's arm. "Ha. If only. But nothing is going on. Absolutely nothing, as you well know. After all, you did have dinner with my roommate and the new sheriff department deputy."

Travis grinned. "Just jerking your chain. I don't care if you put in a hot tub. Besides, it'd probably be good for your leg."

At the mention of his leg, Cash rubbed this thigh. "Probably."

"You know, Caroline mentioned to me before we left that you're walking a lot better. Your limp is barely there anymore. Are you still hurting?"

Cash shrugged, uncomfortable discussing his injuries. "Not much. Now follow me to the back. One more thing to show you."

Cash led them inside to the back bedroom he'd called his own for the first few days. "This room is in terrible shape. The half-bath flooring is almost rotten through. In fact, the entire bath area needs a total rebuild. I was thinking that since I've got to tear it all out anyway, why not go ahead and make it into a full bath? Renovate this entire area, maybe make the room a little larger, a little nicer."

"A little larger and nicer, huh? For who?"

"I don't know. No one in particular. I just thought this house should have a nice master bedroom and bath, but never mind."

"Don't get your panties in wad. Go ahead and knock out a wall or two. Caroline will be thrilled at all you've done." Travis shook his head. "Honestly, I had no idea this place could be renovated like this. I'd actually thought about tearing it down." When Cash looked at him aghast, Travis chuckled. "Yeah, that was my wife's reaction too." They walked into the kitchen. "You really have an eye for this, Cash. Just like that bar you rescued and sent home to Mom and Dad's house. You're good at this. Really, really good. Show me what else you've done."

Once Travis had toured the rest of the house, he seemed pleased with everything that'd been accomplished so far. They rode back to the Halo M ranch, and after promising Caroline a tour of the house soon, Cash headed home. He found a note from Paige on his bed that he'd overlooked earlier.

Date with Marc. Be home later. Leftover meatloaf in fridge.

Well, damn. Yay on the meatloaf, but damn on the date.

Chapter Eight

"Thanks, Marc. I had a lovely time."

"Me too. My friends were crazy about you."

Paige smiled. "That's nice. I enjoyed meeting them."

Marc draped his arm across the back of her car seat. "Since I'm low man on the totem pole, I drew holiday duty through Tuesday, but I'd like to see you again." He caught strands of her hair and rubbed them between his fingers. "I really like you, Paige. I hope you know that."

Paige's heart thudded like stampeding elephants in her ears. A tremor shook her legs. This is what she should want. A stable man. A man who wanted her. A man who saw her as an adult with no memories of her as a child.

He leaned toward her. Paige braced herself for his kiss. Not that he was a bad kisser, because he wasn't.

In fact, he was pretty darned good at it. But no matter how much she wanted to feel the same zing through her blood as when Cash kissed her, Marc's kisses never did more than leave her mouth a little wetter than before.

"I like you too, Marc. Thank you for such a wonderful day. Your friends were great and I loved the fireworks."

He slid the hand that'd been on the back of her seat down to the nape of her neck. He gently pulled her toward him and kissed her. It was a nice kiss. Soft. Non-demanding. Almost reverent with the respect he showed her. He never attacked her mouth as though he couldn't live another minute without her taste. He never gripped her and jerked her against a rigid bulge in his jeans, making her knees weak with need.

In short, he wasn't Cash Montgomery.

"Can I come in?" he asked against her lips.

She shook her head. "Not tonight." Pulling away from him, she smiled. "You have work tomorrow, mister. And it's almost midnight now."

He sighed. "You're right. I knew you'd be good for me." Linking his fingers through hers, he gave them a soft squeeze and then brought them to his lips. "Save Friday night for me. Since I have to work the rest of the weekend, I have the entire next weekend off. Let's go somewhere. Do something special. Just the two of us."

The muscles in her gut twisted into a painful knot. She forced the smile on her face to remain steady. Marc was so nice, such a gentleman. Maybe with a little more time she'd be able to let him into her heart. Her life would be so much calmer with him in it instead of some heart-stopping cowboy. "Sounds wonderfully interesting." She leaned forward and gave him a quick kiss. "Thank you again." She opened the door to leave. "Don't get out. I can walk myself a couple of dozen feet to the door."

"Paige."

She turned back. "Yes?"

"I'm serious. I want to be alone with you. Think about going away for a weekend. Anywhere you want."

"I'll think about it. I promise. Goodnight, Marc."

"Night, Paige."

He waited until she shut her front door before he rumbled down the drive. The living room was dark, as was the rest of the house, except for her bedroom. The lamp beside the living room sofa had been left on. It was throwing just enough light for her to see her way down the hall. She wasn't sure whether to deem Cash considerate for leaving a light on or pissed that he'd left a light on like he was her big brother, or worse, a good friend and considerate roommate.

Which brought up another point. Why wasn't he down here tonight kissing her like she held the breath of life, and without it, he would die?

She flopped onto her bed still fully dressed and stared at the ceiling. The damn man was driving her crazy. One night he's kissing her and the next he's nowhere to be found. Pounding her fists on the mattress, she uttered the dirtiest word she knew. It didn't help.

She climbed off the bed and opened her closet door to kick in her shoes. Cash's belt and silver buckle swung to the side, whapping her wrist. She took the belt off the nail and hung it over the corner of the mirror above her dresser. That memento had traveled with her since the night he'd given it to her. It was one of the few items she owned that she wouldn't sell or trade for anything. Did he even remember giving it to her? He'd probably laugh if he saw it. Think her a silly, sentimental female, which she wasn't. Not by a long shot. But it represented a special night for her, a night that had changed her whole future.

After changing into her pajamas, she crawled between her sheets. As she settled into her foam-gel mattress, she sighed. Why couldn't she fall for someone normal, like Marc Singer? Hell, why couldn't she fall for someone who liked her back? Oh, no. She had to go and fall in love with the most obstinate cowboy God ever put on this earth.

Rolling onto her stomach, she thought about Marc. He was a really super guy. He deserved someone who chose him, not someone who was with him because her number-one choice was a stubborn bullheaded cowboy who needed her whether or not he'd admit it.

And based on that, she needed to tell Marc the truth. She liked him, but she didn't *like* him. Argh. She was going to have to give him the let's-be-friends talk and she *hated* that talk. She'd given it and been on the receiving end of that talk. Both ends sucked.

Flopping onto her back, she resumed her stare of the ceiling. Her door squeaked as it opened a couple of inches. Leaning up on her elbows, did she dare hope it was Cash? That he'd finally come to his senses and come down to her?

Ruby jumped onto the bed, her body so tiny that her landing made no movement. She bumped Paige's arm, followed by a loud purr.

"Hey, sweetheart." Paige sat, pulled the kitten into her lap and began giving Ruby long strokes down her back. "What'd you do today? Have a good day? Did you and Buster play? So what did Cash do while I was gone?"

The cat purred and butted but had no further information about the goings on in the house while Paige was on her date. She and Ruby rubbed noses.

"You're no help at all." Paige fluffed her pillow before lying back down. "You know what I'm going to do, Ruby?" The cat climbed on top of Paige's abdomen and curled into a ball. Paige ran her hand in the cat's fur. "I think I'm going to lasso me a stubborn bullheaded bull rider. He'll never know what hit him until it's too late. What do you think?"

Again, Ruby had no words of wisdom. Just a loud purr of approval.

Paige's alarm beeped at seven. Groaning, she

rolled over and turned it off. Her movement sent Ruby into a purring and head-butting routine.

"Great. Just what I need. A morning cat." Sitting, she stretched. "I am so not a morning person."

Cash's silver buckle caught the morning rays and threw them into her eyes. She squeezed her eyes tight and then she remembered her resolution from last night. Either she needed to excise Cash Montgomery out of her mind and soul or she needed to weasel her way into his. One way or the other, she knew she had to resolve this mental battle before she could move on with her life.

She threw on her robe, brushed her hair and then opened her door. The life-affirming aroma of coffee wafted into her room. Pinch her. She had to be dreaming.

Cash was sitting at the dining room table, a cup of coffee at his elbow, his face hidden by the Sunday *Whispering Springs Gazette*.

"Morning."

Cash lowered the paper enough to look over the top. "Morning." He snapped the paper back into place.

Paige grinned to herself and headed for the kitchen. "Thanks for making coffee."

"No problem." The reply was muted by the newspaper.

While she waited for her toast to pop, she poured a cup of coffee and sipped. A little strong, but not surprising. She knew that most of the coffee the cowboys preferred was as thick as mud.

She carried her toast and coffee into the dining room, which, now that she thought about it, was the first time they'd eaten here instead of the kitchen table.

"What's the occasion?" she asked. When he lowered the paper enough to frown at her, she indicated the table with her cup. "The dining room. I mean, it's nice but we usually sit in the kitchen."

He folded the paper and set it by his plate. "No occasion."

When he started to push his chair back, she said, "Wait. Go with me to church this morning." He started to argue but she cut him off. "They miss you, Cash. You're home but you're not. I mean, you're here in Whispering Springs but you're not seeing your family much."

"Saw Travis yesterday. Will see the rest of the family tomorrow at the annual Bar M cookout and fireworks."

"Sounds like fun. But come with me to church, Cash. I know your mom wants to see you."

"She put you up to this?"

Paige shook her head. "Nope."

"I hate a crowded church. The pews cram packed, hips pressed together, elbows colliding, overwhelming scents from a mixture of perfumes and colognes. Thanks, but no thanks."

"Today's perfect then. Being Memorial Day weekend, the crowd will be sparse. Lots of butt and elbow room. We need to leave here about ten. I'll drive."

He stood. "Of course you will."

At ten when Paige walked into the living room, Cash sat on the sofa dressed in a pair of jeans, a snap shirt with a bolo tie and a jacket. His boots looked freshly polished.

"Well," she said on a sigh. "You clean up right nice, Mr. Montgomery."

He winked at her. "You look pretty spiffy yourself."

Arriving at Whispering Springs United Methodist Church with Cash Montgomery had to be akin to escorting the latest teen idol through a mall. The women all fluffed their hair and pulled back their shoulders. The men had to slap his back or shake his hand. Cash appeared taken aback with the reception, as though he couldn't understand why people would want to cozy up to him.

Sitting alone on the second row, his mother's face lit up as if hit by a spotlight when she got sight of him. The smile that stretched across her mouth produced deep dimples in both her cheeks.

She stood to hug her son. "Cash," she said. "You look wonderful." She clutched his arm as she kissed his cheek. "How are you feeling?"

"Better," he said, and then realized he did feel better. He wasn't in pain anywhere, if his heart ache didn't count. When had his leg stopped hurting all the time? He couldn't remember the last painkiller besides the nightly bedtime aspirin.

"Sit here with me," Jackie Montgomery said, sliding farther down the pew. "You too, Paige. I haven't even greeted you this morning."

Paige smiled. "Good morning, Jackie." She took a seat next to Cash on the pew.

Lane Montgomery entered the church through a side door and slipped into the pew next to his wife. "Morning, son. Paige."

Paige had been right. Attendance was light, to say the least. His parents were the only Montgomerys present beyond him. Olivia, Jason and Travis had apparently skipped this morning, like he wished he could have done.

He hadn't gone to sleep until long after Paige had arrived home from her date. At least the guy hadn't spent the night. Better yet, she hadn't even invited her date into the house. It'd taken every ounce of willpower combined with a dose of cussing to keep him upstairs and away from the front door. Another kiss like the one from Friday night and he'd have been stripping off Paige's clothes as though they were on fire. Then again, another kiss like that and he'd be on fire.

At the moment, his biggest problem was that Paige was simply sitting too close for comfort. Not that she was doing anything but listening to the sermon, but her floral perfume made him want to press his nose into her neck, nibble along her ear, run his tongue down the curve of her chin and then kiss his way down her neck. Her leg touched his when she shifted on the pew. A powerful jolt of sexual awareness surged through his veins. He adjusted his position, but short of running out of the building, he was forced to sit there and let the essence of Paige Ryan permeate every one of his senses.

After the services, his mother grabbed his arm before he could make a run for the door. "I'm glad you came. I was going to call you this afternoon anyway. You are coming tomorrow to the barbeque, right?"

"Wouldn't miss it," Cash said.

"You too, Paige. Lydia did give you our invitation, didn't she?"

A rosy blush bloomed on Paige's cheeks. "She did, but I didn't realize I was supposed to RSVP. I'm so sorry."

Jackie laughed. "No RSVP necessary. Just come on over about three or so."

"Of course. What can I bring?"

His mother thought for a moment and then said, "Pies and cookies. There'll be a herd of kids running around. No one else is bringing cookies and I'm sure we can use another pie or any dessert you want to make. Can you do that?"

Paige grinned. "Cookies are my specialty."

"Excellent." Jackie hugged Cash. "You and Paige want to go to lunch with your dad and me?"

"Thanks, Mom. Maybe some other time."

"Okay. Good to see you, Paige. See you both tomorrow."

Once they were in the car, Cash said, "I still owe you a meal."

"No, you don't."

"Sure I do. I'd planned on taking you out on

Friday, but being that you're so popular, you left me for another man that night."

Paige laughed, the sound lighting a spark inside him. "Yeah. That's my problem. I'm too popular."

Grinning, Cash pointed through the windshield. "Drive. I'm buying lunch."

"Where to?"

"The Rosemont Room. Ever been there?"

Paige shook her head. The Rosemont Room was one of the nicest restaurants in Whispering Springs.

"I figured we got all dressed up and everything. Let's have lunch before we go home."

Paige made a right turn and headed downtown. "If you're paying, I'm eating."

LUNCH WITH CASH WAS LIKE SEEING AN OLD FRIEND. He laughed at her jokes, listened intently while she talked on and on about her new job, and then was ever-so sympathetic when they talked about her parents.

Over steaks and salads, they debated the strengths and weaknesses of every cookie they could name. But they had to agree it might be impossible to find someone who didn't love chocolate chip cookies. Cash claimed he'd never eaten a snickerdoodle cookie, so Paige immediately made a mental note to bake some tonight for his parents' party, along with chocolate chip cookies and a coconut cream pie.

When it came time to order dessert, Cash ordered a *crème brûlée* and two spoons so they could share.

It was the best date Paige had ever been on.

Too bad it wasn't really a date.

When they arrived home, they headed to their separate bedrooms. Paige changed into a pair of shorts that she knew made her butt look great and her *Rope Me, Cowboy* T-shirt. Forgoing shoes, she headed for the kitchen and a few hours of baking. While assembling the needed supplies, she heard Cash tromp down the stairs followed by the click of Buster's nails. The front door slammed, so she could only assume they'd headed for the yard.

Buster was good for Cash. Gave him something to do. Someone who relied on Cash every day. A reason to get exercise multiple times a day, something his injured leg still needed. She couldn't remember the last time Cash had tried to pawn the dog off on someone else. Looked like Buster was here to stay, and she had no problem with that. She'd grown to love the little guy…almost as much as she loved the owner.

She started with the snickerdoodles since they were quick and easy and something new for Cash. She'd just slid the second pan into the oven and was removing the first batch from their pan when the back door opened and Cash and Buster came bounding through. Well, Buster was still bounding. Cash looked as if he'd had enough.

"Hmm. Something smells good," he said. He sat the ball-thrower and a couple of tennis balls on the floor by the door.

"Snickerdoodles."

He snatched a couple of hot ones off the cool rack

and popped one in his mouth. His eyes rolled back as he moaned. "These are wonderful."

"Great. Now stop eating tomorrow's cookies."

"Okay." He grabbed up four more and race-walked from the kitchen.

"I saw that," she called after him, but a broad grin split her lips.

"Saw what?" he answered, but the reply was garbled by a mouth full of hot cookies.

While the snickerdoodles were baking, she started on the chocolate chip cookie dough. She had her back to rest of the kitchen, so when the crinkle of rattling plastic began, she startled. Whipping around to the sound, she furrowed her brow in confusion. Cash had a large roll of clear, thick plastic that he was stapling over the door that led to the back bedroom.

"What are you doing?"

"Aw. How sweet. You're wearing my favorite T-shirt. And I'm covering this door with plastic."

Paige shut her eyes and shook her head. "Yes, I can see that. I meant, why are doing that?"

"You should have asked that then." Cash glanced over at her, a sexy grin on his face.

"Har. Har. Let's try this again. Why are you covering that door?"

The smile on his face was playing havoc with her heart. It raced, skipped and bounced around in response. The guy had sex appeal in spades, and she'd swear he didn't even know it.

"I'm going to be doing a lot of work in here. The bathroom is going to take a total tear out. There's rotten wood in the floor. I want to keep the dust and dirt confined in here as much as possible and out of the kitchen. Plus, I'm adding another exit close to the storm shelter so we can get to it faster if needed."

"Oh." She started the mixer going and then stopped and turned back. "Storm shelter? This house has a storm shelter?"

"Found it totally by accident. Completely out of date but would work in a pinch. I'll show it to you later, but it's on the patio side of the house."

"Cool. Doubt we'll ever need it, but nice to know it's there."

Cash went back to stapling plastic. Paige pulled another pan of cookies from the oven and replaced it with a dough-laden one. All the while, her brain ran over various ways to draw Cash's interest to her. Not as a roommate but as a lover. Maybe if she rolled in the cinnamon and sugar mixture from the snickerdoodles, he'd feel compelled to tongue it all off her. Maybe not exactly the right plan, but she could start there and build on it.

For the rest of the afternoon and into the early evening, she baked to the sound of wood splintering and the occasional cuss word in the adjacent bedroom. She was sliding the last pan of cookies into the oven when the plastic crinkled and a dusty, sawdust-sprinkled Cash stepped through the door.

"Wow. Pigpen has nothing on you."

Cash smiled, his teeth appearing even whiter when surrounded by all the dirt on his face. "Nasty in there. Now you see why I put up the plastic."

"I do and I appreciate it."

"I'm heading for the shower. What do you want to do about dinner?"

Paige eyed the piles of cookies, minus the ones she'd eaten, and her stomach groaned. "I may have eaten too many cookies. I'm not hungry at all."

"What? You wouldn't let me eat them." Cash collected six chocolate chip cookies from the cooling rack. "I'm going to take a shower. How about something easy tonight? Bacon and eggs and toast. I'll even fix it."

"You're on." Standing in the kitchen for the past few hours had Paige's back and legs making their presence known with cramps and aching. "I'm almost done with the cookies. The coconut cream pie is the refrigerator, so hands off. I'll get all this cleaned up and be mostly out of your way when you get back."

She hustled and got everything put away, the cookies stored and was washing the final baking sheet when Cash came back. The spicy scent of Cash's soap swirled around her and she drew in a deep breath.

"Better?" Cash held his arms up and turned.

"It'd be hard to be worse."

He laughed. "Now scoot. The kitchen's mine. I'll holler when dinner's ready."

She saluted. "Aye, aye, Captain Cowboy."

With Cash doing the cooking today—and she did wonder if he could cook since this was the first and only time he'd volunteered—Paige had time for a quick change. If she was going to try to seduce the man, she needed to shower and something sexy to put on. And the sexy outfit had to not look like she was trying to be sexy.

She sighed. Why couldn't she just have liked Marc? It'd have been so much easier.

Digging into her dresser, she found a pair of cut-offs that could never been worn outside the house without fear of public exposure. With those, she put on a white tank top, again eschewing shoes. She'd just finished brushing her hair when she heard his yell.

"Dinner."

Chapter Nine

"Paige. Dinner's ready."

The steak lunch had been great, and usually by this time in the evening, Cash would be starving. But the volume of cookies he'd stolen while Paige's back was turned had put a damper on his appetite.

Plus, ever since church, he couldn't get Paige's scent out of his nose. He'd thought tearing out a rotted, moldy floor would at least replace Paige's floral perfume, but no such luck. It didn't take more than a few seconds to call up the aroma from his mind.

And getting the memory of her thigh pressed to his out of his mind was proving damned near impossible. Just remembering the heat from where she'd touched him sent blood rushing south. And when a man had a hammer and pry bar in his hands ripping up old flooring, he certainly didn't need his Johnson in the way.

"So what's for dinner?"

Cash turned around and almost swallowed his tongue. Good Lord all mighty. Paige wore a pair of shorts that ended no more than three inches below the junction of her thighs. He wondered if the back covered as far down as the curve in her ass. The white wife-beater shirt was so thin that he could see the lace outline on her bra, but he muttered a quick, "Thank you, Jesus" that she wore a bra. As he slid his gaze down her body to the red tips of her naked toes, he knew was going straight to hell.

At least the table would hide his stiff cock. She'd never know the effect she'd had. Keeping his hands off her was the kindest thing he could do for her. For him? Not so much. But definitely better for her.

"Cash? What's wrong?"

He swallowed or tried to. His spit backed up behind the huge ball of lust lodged in his throat, making him choke. He coughed.

"Are you all right?"

He cleared his throat. "Fine. Sorry. I was drinking something and it went down the wrong way."

Yeah. He was drinking her in and it had sure gone down the wrong way…all the way to his dick.

"So." She looked around. "Are we eating in the dining room? I saw plates on the table."

"Yup."

The dining room table was larger than the small table in the kitchen. He could sit farther away.

"Carry this," Cash said, handing her a platter with

bacon and slices of buttered toast. "I'll be right behind you."

When he got to the dining room with the scrambled eggs and jelly, Paige had rearranged the table, moving her plate and utensils from one end of the table to the side next to his place at the other end. There was nothing he could do but sit down beside her. Anything else would have been rude.

Once they were seated, the dining room temperature skyrocketed, or maybe it was just him. He couldn't stop watching her eat. The way her lips wrapped over the fork. The slow way she pulled the fork from her mouth. The way she flicked her tongue out to catch a stray toast crumb or lick the dab of strawberry jelly at the edge.

Breathing became a struggle. Forget even trying to eat. He feared he'd aspirate the eggs into his lungs with his gasps every time Paige did anything remotely connected with her mouth. He had to get his mind somewhere else, but where?

Oh yeah. On why she deserved better than him.

"Let me ask you something," he said.

She took a drink of water then nodded. "Sure."

"Today at lunch, when the waitress asked you if you wanted something from the bar, you sort of looked my way and then said no. I noticed we don't have beer or wine or anything alcoholic in this house. Is all that because of me? Because you think I'm an alcoholic?"

She gasped, her mouth dropped in surprise. Then she shocked him when she started laughing.

"Cash. I'm a grown woman. If I'd wanted a drink, I'd have ordered one. You had nothing to do with why I didn't have a drink today or why I don't have booze in the house. Let me ask you something. Friday night when you examined my tonsils with your tongue, did you taste or smell booze?"

He held her gaze, even as he wanted to dip his head. She'd given a pretty good description of their kiss two days ago.

"Tonsil exam? Really?"

She shrugged and then grinned. "Not that I'm complaining, because I'm not."

Her comment metaphorically slammed him back in his chair. She wasn't upset by the kiss, and if the look on her face was any indication, she wouldn't send him away if he kissed her again. Not that he would.

"To answer your question, no, I didn't smell any booze on you."

"Exactly. I don't drink much, Cash. A glass of wine or champagne at weddings. A beer with pizza. But that's about it. I don't buy it because it'd be flat or stale or whatever between the times I wanted it." Her face grew serious as she leaned toward him. "Were you looking for a drink?"

"So you do think I'm an alcoholic." He tried to put both hurt and anger in his voice. This was great. He could pick a fight, go upstairs and not be faced with all her incredible sexiness.

"Doesn't matter what I think," she said, her voice as smooth, calm and cool as water at daybreak on a lake. "It only matters what *you* think. Do you think you have a drinking problem?"

"You sound like a shrink."

She snorted. "I have a degree in psych, so I probably do. So do you? Have a problem, I mean?"

This time he couldn't hold the gaze. He looked away, out the French doors at the end of the room. "No." He knew he sounded defensive, but damn, did everybody around him think he was a drunk?

"Great." Paige continued to eat as though he'd just told her the weather forecast.

"Okay. Maybe I did. But I don't now." His defensiveness continued. His plan had been to pretend to get angry and leave, but this discussion about his drinking had him actually feeling more than a little testy.

"Okay then. Issue settled. We're a non-drinking house by choice. But if you ever want to talk about what you went through over the past seven months, I'd be glad to listen."

He set his fork on the side of his plate. "I don't want to talk about it. Look, I'm heading up to watch some television. Don't let me hurry you. I'll carry my stuff to the kitchen." He stood and gathered his dirty dishes.

"Cash. Did I say something to upset you?" Her gaze up at him was filled with kindness and, damn it, affection.

"No. I'm sorry. It's just that my brothers are always all over my ass about it and I guess I got a little touchy. Sorry. Finish eating. I'll see you tomorrow."

After putting his dishes in the sink, he headed upstairs with a wave of his hand to Paige still sitting at the table. As soon as Cash stepped on the top floor, Buster came flying up the stairs to join him. He dropped onto his couch, his left leg throbbing, which was unusual as it'd hadn't bothered him much in the last week or so. Buster climbed on the leather sofa, fully aware this was taboo, but tonight, Cash needed the company. Between petting Buster and whatever inane program he could find to watch, he was sure he would be distracted from the pain. At least his penis had gone back into sleep mode.

From downstairs, the sounds of Paige clearing the table and running water in the kitchen floated over the railing. He laid back. What was he going to do about her? His brain said to push her away. But other parts of him wanted to do the opposite. He wanted his brain to win this battle.

The soft tap of a footfall on the lowest step had Buster jumping up and off the sofa. He raced to the top of the stairs and let out a welcoming bark.

"Hi, Buster," Paige said. "I brought you something."

Buster's tail wagged briskly. When he turned away from the step, he was carrying a large rawhide bone. He disappeared into the bedroom with his prize.

"I don't think he's going to share," Paige said. "So I brought you something else."

"Oh?"

"Blueberry cobbler and ice cream. You interested?"

He laughed. It was impossible to be mad at her. Hell, he couldn't even maintain a fake anger.

"Did you heat the cobbler?"

"You're kidding, right? Of course."

He sat up on the couch and she sat down beside him. "Your mom might have mentioned that you had a thing for blueberry cobbler so I thought I'd surprise you."

He took a bite and moaned. "This is better than Mom's. Don't tell her I said that," he added quickly.

"Our little secret. What are you watching?"

"I have no idea. It's just on for noise. Why? Is there something you'd like to see?"

"Nope. I was just going to put some music on instead."

He handed her the remote. "Have at it." But if she put on some love-song station, he'd have to put his foot down. She didn't. She flipped immediately to contemporary country. They ate in silence, him tapping his toe and her bouncing her leg to the music until Faith Hill's "Like We Never Loved At All" started playing. She stood and held out her hand.

"Dance with me, Cash."

He swallowed. This was not a good idea. This was the song that they'd danced to all those years ago. Of course he remembered. Every Faith Hill song dredged up memories of what a shit-heel he'd been. But then she smiled and wiggled her fingers. What else could he do?

He stood, took her hand and pulled her into his arms. They swayed to the music, moving in slow steps around and around. She sighed, her warm breath sliding across his neck like silk.

He tightened his arms to pull her closer and… wham! Excruciating pain shot through his injured leg. His left thigh muscle contracted into an unrelenting spasm.

"Shit." Cash dropped his arms from around Paige and began rubbing his thigh and walking. Every couple of steps, he'd stomp his foot.

"What is it, Cash? What's wrong?"

"Damn leg. Hasn't done this in a while, but when the sonofabitch gets a cramp like this, it takes forever to get it to relax."

"Pull your jeans down and let me rub it."

He eyed her. Let her rub it? Was she serious?

"Don't look at me like that. Pull your pants off and sit down."

When he didn't immediately do what she ordered, she marched into his bedroom. In a minute, she was back with the top sheet of the bed. "Here." She tossed the sheet on the leather sofa. "If you're that bashful, cover up. Although I've seen a penis or two in my life."

She marched away again, but this time to his bathroom and came back with a bottle of hand lotion.

If anything, the muscle spasm was getting worse, not better. Thank goodness, he'd toed off his boots when he'd first sat down to watch television. That left no obstruction to dropping his jeans to the floor. Afterwards, he practically fell back on the sofa.

"Put your leg up on the cushions," she ordered.

Lowering herself to her knees beside the sofa, she

prepared to go to work. She squirted lotion into her hands, rubbed them together and then dug her fingers into the bulging muscle making itself known. Along the edges of the spasm, she worked her thumbs in deep circles, demanding that the cramp give up its control.

The scent of vanilla from the lotion filled the air. He drew in a deep breath and tried to relax.

He studied her, her lower lip sucked between her teeth, her eyes focused on the area giving him so much pain. This was not a Paige Ryan he knew. This was not Doc Ryan's jail bait. This was a take-charge adult female who knew what she was doing when she worked her fingers into the knotted muscle in his leg.

He groaned. Yes, working out the muscle contraction hurt, but there was also something about having Paige on her knees in front of him. His cock liked that idea too. It began to grow hard and move, as though waving for attention too.

"Sorry," Paige said. "I know this hurts, but I think I can get it to let go."

He didn't bother to correct her misinterpretation of his groan. Instead, he grabbed the sheet she'd thrown on the back of the couch and covered himself. If she noticed, she gave no indication. She appeared to be focused on the pain in the leg and nothing else. Should he be pleased that she was so professional and clinical with her touch, or pissed that she hadn't noticed the affect she was having on him?

Since he knew beyond doubt that she deserved

better than he-who-had-no-future, he decided to be relieved.

It was then that pain in his leg lessened. The cramp eased up. Paige must have felt the change because she lifted his leg, slid under and took a seat on the sofa between his calves. After resting his leg across her lap, she retackled the area with a renewed sense of purpose, digging deep with her long fingers, forcing the muscle to do what she wanted.

He couldn't help but be impressed by this strong, forceful woman. She didn't take no from him or his leg spasm.

And then the leg cramp was gone. He blew out a long breath he didn't realize he was holding and settled back against the arm of the couch, his breath coming in short, choppy rasps, his eyes shut in relief. It'd been a bad muscle seizure this time, one of the worst ever. The house renovation was giving him quite a workout, more than he'd had since his run-in with Bad Bob.

"Thanks. That's better. I think you've shown that cramp who's boss," he said with a light chuckle.

"Hmm. Looks like you have another congested area that needs a little attention."

Before her words could register in his brain, she glided her long, soft fingers the rest of the way up his thigh to his throbbing cock. She grasped his length through his briefs.

"Paige. That's probably not a good idea." *Probably?* Hell, definitely.

She ignored his protest, as feeble as it was. She

stroked him, running the length of his dick with her fingers before passing her thumb over the head. His arousal fluid soaked the front of his cotton briefs.

Paige shifted until his foot slipped to the floor, leaving his legs spread. She climbed onto her knees and turned to face him. With a wink and a grin, she snatched the sheet off his groin and tossed it over the back of the sofa. Grasping the elastic waistband of his underwear, she tugged.

"Paige." He leaned up on his elbows, intending to give her a stern look.

She ignored his warning and pulled harder. "Lift your hips." She didn't ask. She demanded.

This most definitely wasn't the timid girl he remembered. As if his hips had separate reasoning, he pushed them up and she yanked his briefs down. His cock sprang out like a bull released from a chute. When she licked her lips, he almost lost it right then.

"Shut up, Cash."

Oh crap. He really liked this take-charge Paige.

She flicked out her tongue and traced the tip along the thick vein on the underside, then swiped the fat surface of her tongue across the slit in the tip of his cock. When she moved her head, her long hair spread over his thighs like a blanket. The flora scent from her shampoo worked its way up his body. His neck wanted to relax, wanted to let his head drop back, but he'd be damned if he could take his gaze off Paige's mouth as it closed over the end of his penis. He hissed in a breath as though her lips had burned his flesh. Inside her mouth, she caressed his rigid cock with moist heat and a wicked tongue doing twists and twirls. When she slid him deeper and he hit her throat, he couldn't contain the long, low moan.

He grabbed the back of the couch with his right hand and the edge of the cushion with his left and squeezed with all his might. Even concentrating on not coming too fast made him want to come.

Then, to torture him a little more, Paige did this humming thing, which vibrated her throat on his cock's head. Holy hell. His hips jerked off the sofa. He drove deeper.

"Holy hell, Paige. I can't take that." Her long red hair tickled his balls when she began moving her mouth up and down his penis, which had reached an almost painfully erect state.

Collecting her hair in one fist, he pulled it off to the side, both to get it off his sensitive balls and to improve his vision. Her lips were red and puffy as she rode him with them. When she sucked, her cheeks pulled inward from the action.

"Babe. Listen," he grunted out in a breathless tone. "I can't…Oh God. That feels so good."

He pulled her hair toward him, forcing her down on his shaft. "Fuck. I can't take much more. Do you hear me?"

Instead of responding, Paige pushed her fingers between his legs and cupped his balls, rolling and fondling them as she continued to draw powerfully on his engorged flesh.

He ceded the battle to her and gave himself over to the oncoming orgasm. It didn't take but a couple of additional hip thrusts and an electrical jolt hit his system as he came.

When his dick finally finished jerking, Paige released him from her mouth.

"Here's the deal, slick," she said with a lift of an eyebrow. "I'm still attracted to you and, if I'm reading your kisses accurately, the feeling is mutual." She sat back on her heels with a sigh. "I want to finish what we started seven years ago. Don't freak out," she added quickly when he opened his mouth to speak. "I'm not looking for long-term or asking for a commitment. Come fall, school's going to be time consuming and tough. I won't have the time or the energy for a relationship." She shrugged. "So for as long as it lasts, I propose roommates with benefits. What do you say?"

Say? He couldn't say anything. Who was this creature between his legs? It wasn't the sweet girl who'd blushed when he'd kissed her at sixteen, that was for sure. And that thing she did with her tongue? Who the hell had taught her that? He'd probably kill the bastard if he ever found out. Then again, maybe not, because oh my God, had she been a good student.

"Cash? Don't you have anything to say?" she asked with a frown.

He shook his head.

"Good." Her smiled covered her puffy lips…lips that'd just given him the best head of his life. "What do you think?"

Cash cleared his throat and pulled to a sitting position. "What about Marc Singer?"

She did that cute little eyebrow lift again. "What about him?"

"Aren't you seeing him?"

"Ah. Seeing, yes. Sleeping with, no. I don't sleep with multiple partners at one time. In fact, as long as we are lovers, I'd have to insist you restrict your sexual activities to just me."

"Don't you think the guy you're seeing would mind if he finds out you're sleeping with your roommate?"

She shrugged. "If Marc and I get serious enough to move it to the bedroom, then we—you and I—are done. Like I said, I like it one-on-one." She started to slide from the couch and stopped. "In fact, the same deal your way. If you start seeing someone—wait. You're not involved with anyone right now, are you?"

He shook his head. "Nope."

"Great. Then when and if you do get involved with anyone, just say the word and we're done. Okay?" She stood and looked down at him. "No harm. No foul."

Her searing gaze was like staring into the blazing sun. Okay? He was stunned. Bumfuzzled, as his grandpa used to say.

"Before I decide one way or the other, I want to make sure we're clear on a few points. We have no future. There is no *us*. No long-term happy-ever-after. This isn't a fairy tale, Paige. It's real life." He hated sounding so hard, so brusque, but she had to understand he had nothing to offer her. "If we do this, it's just sex. Not making love or any other pretty label you might want to put on it. If it lasts through the summer, fine. We'll go our separate ways when you leave for school. If either of us wants out before then, it's over. No questions. No tears. No regrets."

Her smile might have faltered for just a second and a look of uncertainty might have flashed across her face, but just for a second. Then she seemed to regroup.

"Fine," she said.

"Fine. Let's both sleep on it and talk about it tomorrow."

She gave him a short head bob, turned her back to him and walked away. "Oh. And you owe me an orgasm," she said over her shoulder as she took the first step down.

Fuck a duck. Bad, *bad* idea.

And yet a very interesting idea.

Chapter Ten

Paige skated down the stairs to her room after making the most outrageous proposition of her life. Her heart jackhammered her chest wall. Had he seen how absolutely terrified she'd been the whole time? Her teeth had been chattering so hard during oral sex that at one time she feared she'd bite him. For him to say he'd think about it? That didn't do much for her confidence.

And another sticky wicket was Travis's one thousand dollars per month. She hadn't deposited or cashed the checks from April or May. Honestly, she'd only agreed to take the money because she'd still been so mad at Cash for moving into her house. She and Leo had both received sizeable inheritances when their parents died, enough that she could attend graduate school without taking out a student loan, but not enough to set her up for life. She'd still have to work.

Her parents hadn't had that large of an estate to pass down.

She sighed. Decision made. Tomorrow, regardless of Cash's answer, she would return those checks to Travis and ask him to send no more.

Once she'd climbed into bed, her mind turned into a vicious bitch, taunting her with different scenarios of how he would reject her again. The worst one was of him laughing while telling others about her desperate attempt to get him to sleep with her. She tossed and turned like a pig on a spit.

The annoying jangle of her phone alarm woke her at nine. The last time she'd looked at the clock it'd been close to four, so she'd gotten at least a few hours of sleep. In the harsh reality of daylight, embarrassment took root inside her. How would she be able to face Cash this morning? What would she say? Should she just pretend everything was normal and wait for him to broach the subject? Or take the bull by the horns and ask for his answer?

As luck would have it, she didn't have to make any decisions. When she got to the kitchen, the coffee was waiting along with a note.

P

Dad called early this morning and I had to go over to Bar M to help set up for today. I'll see you there.

C

p.s. I've made a decision about our discussion last night.

Super. He'd made a decision but didn't want to leave it in a note. That did not bode well. Obviously, he was going to say no and wanted to tell her in person so he could explain.

Damn.

She wadded up the note and tossed it in the trash. A swell of disappointment swamped her soul. And as badly as she didn't want to cry, she couldn't hold back. Tears filled her eyes and rolled down her face. She swiped at them with her hand, angry at Cash for rejecting her *again* and furious at herself for caring that he had.

After a good ten-minute pity party, she washed her face at the kitchen sink, dried it and got out the ingredients for another coconut cream pie. A glance in the refrigerator told her Cash had eaten coconut cream pie for breakfast before leaving. There was no way she would take a half-eaten pie over. And as long as she had the oven hot, she also baked a blueberry cobbler to take.

She spent the rest of the morning running a vacuum and dusting and cleaning up the mess she'd made in the kitchen. At two, she loaded cookies and pies into her car and headed over to the Bar M.

Traffic was surprisingly heavy on their little back road. When she turned into Bar M, she saw why. Parked cars lined the drive from the road to the house. Since there was no way she could carry all this food that distance, she drove on up, intending to unload and drive back down to find a parking place. As luck would have it, she pulled in behind a sheriff's department car. Marc Singer opened the driver's door and climbed out.

"Am I glad to see you," she called out the window.

He pivoted at her voice and smiled. "Hi, Paige. Glad to see me, huh?" He headed back to where she parked. "Need a hand with something?"

"Please. Can you carry in these for me?" She handed him the two pies while she got the large container of cookies. "It'll save me a second trip."

"Happy to." He balanced a pie in each hand. "What kind?" He nodded to the foil-covered dishes.

"Coconut cream pie and blueberry cobbler."

"You're awesome." He leaned over and gave her a quick kiss. "You remembered that blueberry cobbler is my favorite."

No. She didn't even remember a conversation about blueberry cobbler. "Let me know if you enjoy it." She looked at him with a puckered brow. "I thought you had to work today."

"I am at work. Since it seems like most of the county is out here, the sheriff stationed me in the area. Last year, there was a heck of a fight between a couple of drunks over which one was more patriotic."

They both laughed.

"So will I get to see you later?" Marc asked. "Maybe we can eat some of this blueberry cobbler together."

Once again, Paige's heart took off at a race-walk pace. "Maybe. I'll look for you." They walked into the house and set their offerings on the counter. "Thanks again for your help, Marc."

He kissed her cheek. "I'll catch up with you."

As he was brushing her cheek with his lips, the

kitchen door opened and Jackie Montgomery entered. "Excuse me," she said with a grin. "I'll just go out and knock before I come into my kitchen."

Marc chuckled while Paige felt a hot flash rise in her neck.

"Looking good, Jackie," Marc said. "I'd be giving you a kiss too but I've seen Lane's right hook."

Jackie rolled her eyes. "Please. I'm old enough to be your mother," she said, but Paige could see she was flattered by Marc's words.

"I'm gone." He turned toward Paige and brushed a lock of hair over her shoulder. "I'll see you later."

As soon as he left the kitchen, Jackie looked at Paige. "Sorry for the interruption."

"You didn't interrupt anything. I promise. Marc was just helping me bring in stuff from my car."

Jackie arched an eyebrow. "Can't say that I'm disappointed then. I was kind of hoping you and Cash were getting together." She sighed. "I'd really love to see that boy settle down and get happy."

Paige gulped. She wasn't sure how to respond but was saved when Olivia, Cash's sister, walked in.

"Okay, Mom. Here's the stuffed potatoes. Mitch is behind me with buns. Hi, Paige. How's it going?"

Latching on to the reprieve, Paige smiled. "Hi, Olivia. Going great. I'm just going to head outside to mingle. Talk to you later."

She made her escape before she blurted out that she and Cash would never get together because he didn't want her.

The area around the house was packed with

people milling around. Across the yard, her brother, Leo, stood talking to a woman Paige didn't know. He waved then kept talking to his female friend. All around her were people she'd come to know over the past ten months. All the Montgomerys, of course. The Milholens and Rowes from church. The town librarian, Susie Wilson, who was talking animatedly with Frank White, the town butcher. Paige made her way through the crowd, stopping to say hi or inquire about children and then moving on.

"Looking for me?"

Turning toward the voice, she smiled. "Hi again," she said to Marc. "No, but your timing is great." She slipped her arm through his. "I wanted to talk to you about something."

"Sure. Here?" He made a head gesture to area around them.

"No. Let's step to some place a little more private."

He led her out of the crowd and around a tall privet hedge. "This better?"

"Yes."

"I'm hoping you've asked me here to tell me where we're going this weekend."

His words sent a ripple of regret through her. Why couldn't she fall for someone like him?

"No. Not exactly." She squeezed his arm then pulled hers free.

"There's someone else."

She shrugged. "Yes and no."

He shook his head. "Cash isn't exactly a roommate, is he?"

"No, he's just a roommate."

There must have been something in her expression because Marc touched her cheek with his fingers. "But you want more than that with him, right?"

"I don't know," she said on a long exhale. "I think I do." Their gazes met. "I'm sorry, Marc. It's just not right for me to keep seeing you when my heart is focused elsewhere."

He caressed her cheek and she found herself leaning into his touch. "I'm sorry too. I hope you find what you want." He gave her a sad smile and then kissed her. "I wish it was me."

"Me too."

"If anything changes, know that I'll be waiting. I won't wait forever but—"

"Excuse me? Am I interrupting?"

Paige jumped and whirled around. Cash stood at the end of the hedge looking quite pissed off.

"No, not at all," Marc replied, his voice calm and collected.

Paige, on the other hand, was far from calm or collected. "Oh, hi. We were, um, just talking." The shaky, squeaky tone of her voice had her flinching with embarrassment. But why should she be embarrassed? First, she wasn't doing anything wrong. Second, he didn't have any claim to her since he was totally going to blow her off. And third…well, she couldn't think of a third, but still.

"If you've got a minute, roomie, I've got something I want to show you."

Paige glanced at Marc.

"Go on. I think we've finished our conversation anyway."

"Thanks, Marc. I'll see you later."

"Yeah. Thanks." Cash grabbed her hand and pulled her along behind him.

"Where are we going?"

"Just wait. You'll love it."

No one appeared to notice as she was shanghaied and tugged through the crowd toward the barn. People just smiled or gave a nod of hello. This is probably how people got kidnapped every day. Nobody noticing, except to wave.

"Cash."

"Wait." He continued their trek until they reached the barn doors. Opening a door, he gestured her inside. As soon as she was inside, he followed and shut the door behind him.

"Best people-watching spot on the whole ranch," he said. "C'mon."

She followed him to a ladder. There, he placed a small stool at the base. "Go on. Climb up."

She moved her gaze up the ladder. "Hay loft?"

"Yep. Go on. Climb. I'm right behind you. Use the small step if that'll help with the first rung."

"Please. Give me break. I don't need that." Grabbing hold of the third rung, she hit the first step on the ladder and shimmied up into the loft with ease. Below her, she heard a clank and a thud as though Cash were moving things. But in a moment, his head popped through the opening and he joined her.

"Over here." He walked over to an opening used to load or unload hay from the loft. He pushed open the door. Spread out below was Bar M Ranch. Guests laughed and drank as they walked and mingled on the immediate property.

Paige stood in the opening, holding on to the frame and took in the scene below. "Oh. This is awesome."

"I know." Cash stood behind her, his position an identical pose. The heat from his chest radiated to her back, and for a moment, Paige closed her eyes and enjoyed the sensation.

"Being the youngest sucks sometimes," Cash continued, "like when I couldn't go to one of my brothers' parties because I was too young. So I'd climb up here and watch." He chuckled. "Oh, the education I received."

She glanced over her shoulder into his silver-blue eyes. "Do tell."

"I'll not only tell you, but later I'd be willing to demonstrate some of that learning," he said with a pump of his eyebrows. "For now, let's see who we know." He pointed to the left. "That's your brother. Do you know the woman he's talking to?"

Paige focused on the woman Leo had cornered. "No. Who is she?"

"Local debutante. Elsie Belle Lambert. I think she divorced husband number three last year. Could be four," he said with a shrug. "I lose count. She's on the husband prowl. You might want to warn Leo."

"Forget it. I stay out of his love life." She looked across the yard. "Who's that?"

Cash followed Paige's pointed finger. "That's Reno Montgomery. My cousin. The woman he's talking to is Magda Hobbs, Mitch and Olivia's housekeeper."

"I recognized Magda. That's why I asked."

He rested his chin on her shoulder. "Darren, his brother, is around here somewhere, I'm sure." He leaned to the right. "There he is." He pointed at a dark-haired man dressed like everyone else in jeans, boots, snap shirt and hat. "He's talking to his sister, KC. Do you know her?"

"I've met her. Don't really know her."

As they watched the tableau playing out below, Cash's lips caressed her ear as he spoke. "There's another reason I brought you up here."

"Oh?" Her heart and lungs began vying for fastest rate.

"I wanted to give you my answer to your proposition last night." He turned her to face him. "I would have at breakfast if Dad hadn't called me over so early this morning." Lacing his fingers through hers, he brought her hand up to his lips and kissed her knuckles. "Not that there was anything to think about. We were both quite clear that this fling, or sex, or whatever you want to call it, is temporary. Neither of us is looking down the road at a future together, right?"

She nodded. "That's right." She was such a liar,

liar pants on fire that it was a divine miracle the straw around them didn't burst into flames.

He leaned forward and kissed her. At first it was a soft kiss, a tender meeting of lips. Then he pulled back and caught her gaze. "You saw the scars on my legs last night. There're more on my chest and back. They're ugly."

"I don't care, Cash." She reached out and jerked the snaps running down the front of his shirt. Sliding her hands between the open edges, she glided her palms across the muscles and sinew of his chest to his sides, then walked her fingers down to the ridges of his abdomen. "We all have scars. Yours just happen to be on the outside." She leaned over to trace the tip of her tongue along the scar on the right side of his abdomen until she reached his belly button, where she used her tongue to outline the edges.

Cash sucked in his breath as he simultaneously sucked in his abdomen. Threading his fingers through her red tresses, he pulled her back up to his mouth for a hard, wet and deep kiss. He pushed his tongue into her mouth, running it around in circles, licking the inside of her cheek, her teeth.

Paige groaned, which seemed to excite Cash. He gently pushed her onto her back into the hay scattered on the floor.

"Wait. What if someone can see us?"

"Only if they're in a hot air balloon," he said, nibbling around the edge of her chin. "But scoot back two feet if it makes you feel better."

She laughed but scooted back a couple of feet.

Then she shoved him off her. She grabbed the hem of her shirt, pulled it up and off and tossed it over a bale of hay.

"Hold on. Let me grab something that'll make this a little more comfortable."

Cash stood, walked to the other end of the loft and brought a blanket back with him.

"Aren't you the smart one," Paige said, toeing off her boots. "That hay itches like crazy. I was getting ready to put you on the bottom."

He laughed as he spread out the blanket. "This ain't my first rodeo." He yanked his shirt off and tossed it on top of hers. Then he dropped to his knees beside her, catching her face in his hands. "You are still the most gorgeous woman I've ever known." He kissed her, following her onto the blanket until he was on top.

He started with her mouth and worked his way down her body. He kissed and nibbled his way down her neck and chest until he reached the top of her bra. Catching the tip of her breast in his mouth, his hot breath seeped through the thin lace. She shivered and rolled to the side so he could reach the clasp in the back. A flick and the bra's band loosened. Cash shoved it up and wrapped his lips around her nipple, sucking and drawing it deep into his mouth using his tongue to work her flesh. Paige became lost in the suck, draw, lick, suck, draw, lick of his delicious mouth.

She snaked a leg around his calf and jutted her hips up, grinding against his rigid shaft. Shoving a hand between them, she went to work on his belt, unfastening it to get to the metal button of his jeans. She pushed the metal through the buttonhole and then stopped.

"Wait. You have a condom? 'Cause I don't."

"Yep. Front left pocket."

"Right. Not your first rodeo."

He chuckled until she wiggled her hand into his tight jeans pocket. His amusement abruptly ended when she stopped digging for the condom long enough to caress his cock through the pocket material. When she withdrew her hand, she pulled the foil packet out and laid it on a bale of hay beside her.

He pushed her onto her back and began slowly dragging the tip of his tongue down her abdomen. When he dipped into her belly button, she sucked in her gut in reflex.

"You taste so good," he said against her skin, his lips brushing her flesh like butterfly wings. "But I'm thinking you'll taste even better lower."

Sliding down her legs to her feet, he undid her jeans and pulled both her jeans and her panties down her legs and off.

"Spread your legs for me," he ordered. He licked her ankle, then up the inside of her leg. "Wider. Let me look at you." She spread her legs wider and he moved farther up her leg with his mouth and tongue. Pressing his nose to her sex, he inhaled deeply. "I can smell how much you want this, want me."

His deep, guttural tone liquefied her insides, sent every drop of moisture flowing toward Cash and his hot breath. She lifted her hips, thrusting against his mouth.

He sucked on her flesh, drawing her engorged tissues between his lips. He flicked his tongue against her nub, stabbing it, licking, stabbing. She felt his hand as he slid it up her thigh, then his fingers when he probed her entrance. When he pushed two fingers inside her canal, she moaned and moved on them.

Her sex throbbed and ached for relief. Her hips moved against his mouth and hand without conscious thought on her part. Every cell in her mind was focused between her thighs and the blond-haired man there.

The swirl of tension inside whipped around like a tornado, pulling everything inside its vortex. She grabbed his head, holding him exactly where she wanted him. Her hips gyrated. The pressure grew almost painful and then exploded inside her. White lights flashed behind her eyelids as wave after wave of intense pleasure rippled through her.

When the orgasm finally faded, tears dampened her cheeks.

"Are you okay? Hey. Babe. You're crying."

She laughed and wiped at the wetness on her face. "I'm fine. It was…" She sighed. "I needed that." Opening one eye, she glanced at him. "A little over-dressed for this party, aren't you, cowboy?"

Cash chuckled and stood. He shucked his jeans and retrieved the condom and rolled it down his engorged penis.

"How's this?" he said.

"Perfect. C'mon. Let me show you how I ride a cowboy."

As soon as his knees touched the blanket, Paige used one finger to push him onto his back. Tossing a leg over him, she lowered herself onto his stiff staff. He thrust up with his hips, driving himself deep inside. As she glided up and down, he dug his fingers into the flesh of her hips. Every time he slammed into her, a whirl of growing energy shot through her, driving her closer to the ultimate high she sought. And just as she was seconds from her release, he raised her off his cock. She whimpered in frustration.

The muscles in his cheeks were tense and his voice gravelly as he said, "Stand up. Turn around and put your hands here." He indicated a hay bale with a lift of his chin.

As he demanded, she stood and stretched her hands out on the scratchy bale.

"Bend over," he said.

The roughness of his tone fired a bolt of lightning through her system. She shivered and leaned forward, her bare ass rising into the air.

"Oh, baby," he said. "That's looking nice."

He stroked his hands over her rear and then ran a finger down her crack. When she moaned, he pushed her shoulders down closer to the hay, propelling her bottom even higher.

"Oh, yeah. That's it," he said and rammed into her.

She arched her back as she tried to get more leverage. He pulled back and slammed again and again.

The sound of his balls slapping her flesh echoed around her and she thought it might be the most erotic thing she'd ever heard.

He slid a hand around her hip, found her clit and pressed. Between the friction of his cock against her vaginal walls, the slap of flesh against flesh and the continued manipulation of her sensitive nub, she didn't stand of chance of lasting very long.

The orgasm slammed through her like a jet on take-off. She bowed her back with a long groan as her muscles shook and twitched with pleasure. A couple of quick thrusts and Cash followed her over the edge. His hot, damp chest adhered to her back as he blew long breaths.

"Damn, Paige."

"I know," she gasped out. "I—"

He clamped his hand over her mouth. When she looked at him over her shoulder, he put one finger over his lips for her to be quiet.

"C'mon, Caroline. Mom's got the kids occupied. Let me show you the best view of the…damn."

"What's wrong, honey? Did you step on something?"

"No. I just remembered. You haven't seen my old bedroom, have you?"

"What has gotten in to you?"

"C'mon, babe. I got a better spot." Then it sounded like he raised his voice so anyone else in the barn would hear. "I've got soft sheets that won't have hay prickling me in the back."

The door downstairs banged shut. Paige giggled

and then sneezed. The door downstairs creaked open. "Bless you." The door slammed shut again.

Mortification at being discovered shot heat up Paige's neck. She dropped her gaze toward the dusty floor as Cash laughed.

"I don't think you're the first Montgomery to sneak a gal into the loft," Paige said.

"How do you think I learned about it? Remember? I spied on my brothers' parties. Let's just say, it was quite an education."

The loud gong of a bell rang out from the yard.

"Dinner's ready," Cash said. "Get dressed. We want to beat my brothers to the chow."

Paige hustled around the loft, finding the various pieces of her clothes tossed over the bales of hay. Dressed, they headed for the ladder.

"Wait. Let me go first," Cash said.

"Why?"

"Well, there might be a couple of things leaning against the ladder down there."

She looked over the lip of the floor and saw a pitchfork with its handle shoved through the lower rungs and a shovel with a bucket upright on its handle balanced against the pitchfork tines.

"What the ...?"

He started down the ladder but looked up with a grin. "Jason's signal to Travis that he's got a girl up here." She could hear him laughing as he climbed down.

Later, with plates heaped with ribs, baked-potato salad, beans, coleslaw and bread, Cash and Paige found spots at a picnic table with Jason and Lydia. She sat by Jason and Cash slipped in on the other side next to Lydia.

"Hey, beautiful," he said, nuzzling his future sister-in-law's neck.

"Hands off, bro," Jason said, his mouth full of rib meat with absolutely no threat in his voice.

Cash laughed. "Dad outdid himself this year." He gnawed on the thick meat of a rib. ""But wait until you have some of Paige's pie." He grinned, barbeque sauce smeared on his lips.

"Thanks. I um, noticed, you might have had a slice of pie for breakfast. Especially since there was less than half of the pie left."

"Guilty as charged. I'm a growing boy."

"Yeah, growing faster in the gut than height," Jason said.

"Scoot over." The deep bass voice was sexy as hell and Paige knew it immediately. Travis, Cash's brother. The one who'd almost discovered their little love nest this afternoon.

Cash moved closer to Lydia and Travis climbed onto the bench, plopping a plate groaning with meat on the table. Caroline slipped in next to Paige.

"Well, hell, big bro," Jason said. "You in competition with Cash over who can eat the most?"

"Surprised you're not hungrier," Travis growled. "I mean, after all that afternoon loft activity."

Paige choked on the potato salad she'd just forked into her mouth. Caroline patted Paige's back.
"You okay?"

Paige nodded and took a sip of water, her gaze meeting the amused look Cash gave her.

"What are you talking about?" Jason said.

"Nothing. Ignore my husband," Caroline said. "Lack of sleep has him a tad cranky."

"I'm not cranky. I'm—"

"Cranky," his wife interjected. "Your mom used his old room as nursery for the kids and Travis missed his nap."

Paige bit her lip to keep from laughing.

After pies and cakes had been demolished under the guise of not hurting the cooks' feelings, the men threw age out the window and headed to a field for a game of flag football. After the second down, the flags were gone and it was every man for himself.

The women pulled up folding chairs and cheered from the sidelines.

"None of those guys are going to be able to walk tomorrow," Caroline said with a laugh. "Stiff backs. Sore legs. Bruises." She looked at Lydia. "Our office is going to be busy tomorrow."

"With just these guys?" Paige asked with a frown. "There are only about thirty-six or so out there."

"That's true," Lydia replied. "But count up how many of them are single. Our waiting room will suddenly become the hot place to meet a guy."

Paige giggled. "I may need to be in the lobby doing triage tomorrow."

Caroline snorted.

Paige settled back in her chair and watched Cash. Yes, he was limping, but he was out there fighting with the rest of them. He looked particularly happy when he tackled Marc Singer, who'd joined the game after end of his shift.

After the winning touchdown was scored, the entire population of the ranch came alive with activity as people began loading chairs, coolers and people into the back of trucks, and driving through an open gate and through a pasture.

"Where's everybody going?" Paige asked.

"Fireworks," Cash said. "Grab the chair you're in. I loaded a cooler in the truck this morning."

"I hope you scraped out the first layer of trash from inside."

He grinned. "Maybe, but you'll never know if you don't hurry up. Hand me your chair."

"I can carry it."

"I know you can, but I want to."

Paige's heart sighed. "Okay. Here you go." She stood, collapsed her chair and handed it to Cash.

"Now hurry or we won't get a good seat."

"A good seat for fireworks? Don't they go up into the sky and go boom where we can all see them?"

"Heck, not the fireworks. A good place where we can make-out during the fireworks."

Paige laughed and started running toward his truck. "Why are you so slow?" she called over her shoulder.

Chapter Eleven

June hit Whisper Springs with a slap of heat and humidity. Cash's work on the house continued, albeit a little slower. Paige found herself conflicted every morning…wanting to stay in bed with Cash and yet excited to go to work.

She'd been on target when she'd told her brother it'd been a long time since she'd used her nursing education. It'd taken her most of the month to get comfortable with all the medical and nursing knowledge that scrolled through her brain every day. But she loved it.

Her only regret was knowing that summer was passing quickly and soon she'd be spending a year in university housing to complete her nurse-practitioner education. That meant leaving a job she loved and a man she loved even more.

But not going wasn't an option either. When she graduated, she'd be able to come back to Whispering

Springs Medical Clinic and assume a more active role. She looked forward to that.

A year wasn't that long to be away. She be back seeing the patients and treating their problems before she knew it.

And she and Cash had that stupid agreement. No long-term commitments. No-harm, no-foul bullshit. What had she been thinking?

Oh yeah. She'd been thinking she wanted a stubborn, shaggy-headed cowboy. Now, she hated the damn agreement, even if she'd been the one to propose it. Somewhere deep inside, she'd thought he'd change his mind, but so far he'd appeared perfectly content with their arrangement.

Was it the old adage, *why buy the cow when you can get your milk for free?*

The second week she'd worked at Whispering Springs Medical Clinic, she'd gone with Lydia to see patients at the Greenwood Assisted Living Center, which was more a skilled-care facility than an assisted-living facility. However, the patients were well cared for by a first-rate staff. She'd come to love those visits. By the end of June, she'd been making some of the medical visits solo, calling Lydia or Caroline only if a patient had a problem she couldn't handle.

Very quickly, one of the oldest patients there, ninety-four-year-old Mrs. Hagan became her favorite. Irene Hagan always had a funny story or joke to tell. Her family didn't live close and didn't get to visit except a couple of times a month. That didn't seem to faze her. She'd gotten an iPad and learned how to talk with her grandchildren and great-grandchildren via the internet. Having met most of her family through Mrs. Hagan's computer screen, Paige never pictured any of them with arms and legs, just big talking heads. Mrs. Hagan thought that was the funniest thing Paige had ever said.

The last Monday in June, Paige arrived at Greenwood with a bouquet of flowers for the nurses' station. A collection of people stood in the hall outside Mrs. Hagan's room. As she made her way down the hall and the huddle turned toward her, she recognized most of the faces. Mrs. Hagan's family. But on a Monday?

"Hello. I'm Paige Ryan."

Diane Hagan Lee held out her hand. "I'd know your face anywhere."

Paige smiled and shook her hand. "Yours too. Funny but I've only seen you as faces on your mother's screen."

Diane smiled. "I know. Mom told me. Big talking heads."

The group around Diane chuckled at the comment. Seems Mrs. Hagan had shared Paige's comment with the entire family.

"I'm a little surprised to find all of you here," Paige said. "Is your mom okay? We didn't get a call at the office that there was a problem."

"Oh, there isn't. Today is Mom's ninety-fifth birthday. We came to surprise her. We're taking her out to a dinner celebration."

"How thoughtful. I know she'll love it." Paige

addressed the group. "It's so nice to see all of you. Have a wonderful night out."

After her rounds at Greenwood, Paige was sitting in her car when the Hagan gang filed out. They were loud and noisy and it hit her how much she missed her own parents. She checked the date and was suddenly overwhelmed with grief.

The month had slid away without her noticing. The job. Cash. The planned move. Somehow she'd missed that today was the day her parents had died.

She choked on a sob. Resting her head on her steering wheel, she would have sworn she could hear her mother's voice. "Don't cry, baby. You have a wonderful life ahead of you. What's done is in the past. You can only affect the future. Your dad and I are proud of you. Now dry those tears and get home to that man you're so crazy about."

Even though she knew the voice was only in her head, she couldn't help but smile. *Thanks, Mom.*

That night, Cash was warm and considerate as he held her. They shared their favorite memories of her parents and the crazy and funny stories from the days riding the circuit. She laughed a lot. Cried a couple of tears, but mostly she laughed.

When she awoke the next morning, still wrapped in Cash's arms, she gave a silent thanks for having him in her life right now. Without him, yesterday would have been torture. Instead, it had turned into a lovely evening of shared memories and a shared past.

She adored her only living family members, Leo and her Uncle James, but neither of them had been on the rodeo circuit with her and her parents. Visits along the way, sure, but visits were like a vacation, not everyday life.

Cash had been on the road with them sharing everyday events, like the day the radiator had blown on her truck and left her stranded for two hours in Wyoming. Or on her fourteenth birthday when the rodeo bullfighters had loaned her their pancake make-up, red lipstick and baggy clothes so she could go into the arena with them. Needless to say, she was kept far away from any activity. Still, being in the arena had been thrilling, and Cash had been there to see it, just as her parents had.

She could tell people her life history, but having someone who'd been there, who'd seen what she'd seen and experienced what she'd experienced brought a totally different dynamic to a conversation. Cash gave her something no one else could right now—a connection to her past. She'd needed that connection, and there weren't many people who could provide it.

When Paige arrived home the next evening, she sat in her car for a couple of minutes soaking in the changes in the house. When she and Ruby had first arrived, the two-story house had looked dead. Peeling external paint. Dirty windows. Crooked brown shutters. Window baskets growing whatever wild grass seeds blew in.

Now the house gleamed with white paint. The shutters were red and straight. A matching red front door greeted visitors. The dirty, cobweb-infested porch with its nasty railings were clean and white. Two rocking chairs graced what had been an empty porch. Today, two fluffy green fern baskets had been hung, completing the picture of a house alive with energy and personality. The grass in the yard needed mowing, but it still looked and felt like home to her.

Cash had the touch. He'd brought this dead old house back to life, and she'd bet he could do that for other houses. Was he was aware of his talent? Aware of how physically far his mind and body come in only ten weeks?

Back in April when she'd run into him at Leo's, his skin had been a wrinkled-filled and an unattractive pasty gray. His eyes, what little she'd seen, had been bloodshot and unfocused. And while he'd still retained his muscular undertone, he'd appeared weak and unsteady, the effect magnified by his limp.

Now, at the end of June, he didn't resemble that man at all. He was the man she'd known on the rodeo circuit. Strong. Decisive. Confident. His sense of humor was back. His color was back. If she didn't know about his injuries, she'd have never noticed the very slight limp.

He'd rebuilt much of himself just as he had the house, and she was so proud and thrilled for him.

She let herself into a quiet house. The aroma of baking potatoes filled the downstairs.

"Cash. You here?"

"Upstairs. Come on up."

A smile crawled across her lips when she hit the landing. Curled up together on the leather sofa, Ruby and Buster both wagged tails at her arrival, but neither deemed her arrival important enough to move.

Dressing in a pair of shorts, a PBR T-shirt and barefoot, Cash was stretched out in his recliner while Judge Judy played on the television. His blond hair, at least a month past needing a cut, fell over his brow. Her heart skipped at the sight of the man she adored smiling at her.

"Judge Judy?"

Cash shrugged with a guilty grin. "Not my fault. It's what Ruby and Buster want to watch every afternoon."

She glanced at the animals. Ruby was washing her hind leg while Buster's eyes were shut.

"Hmm. Yes, I can see their fascination."

He laughed and patted the arm of the chair. As soon as her butt hit the arm, he pulled her into his lap. There was a tug in her gut as her bottom settle into his lap.

"Have a nice day?"

"I did. I've really gotten attached to some of our regular patients."

"So you're still liking the work?"

She nodded. "Loving it."

"Still heading off to the big D for school in the fall?"

"Yep. Why all the questions?"

"I got you a present."

She wasn't sure if that was a change of subject or if the questions were somehow related.

"A present?" She slid her hips side-to-side over his growing erection. "I think I can feel your present."

He chuckled. "That present's for later. Reach beside the chair. You should feel a box."

When she leaned over, her rear rose in the air. Cash ran his hand over her ass cheeks before lightly biting the left one.

"Hey!" she said indignantly, but her voice held no threat.

"Sorry. I couldn't resist. Go on. Lean over. I promise not to bite."

She gave him a skeptical look but leaned over. He didn't bite, but his hands roamed. Her finger touched the corner of a box, which she pulled back into his lap. Wrapped in a big red satin bow, the white box was about two feet long and a foot wide.

"What's this for?"

He lifted a shoulder as a cute blush pinked his cheeks. "No reason. Just saw it. Thought you might like it."

After opening the lid and pulling away the freshly folded tissue paper, she touched soft, silky material. She whipped it from the box. A long, royal-blue silk robe hung from her fingers. On the back was an orange and yellow sunset.

"Oh, Cash. It's beautiful. The sunset looks like the one we get every evening. Thank you. I'll think of you every time I wear it." She kissed him and then hopped from his lap. "I want to try this on right now."

Cash lowered his feet to the floor. "I've got to check dinner anyway."

"What are we having?"

"Baked potatoes, rolls, salad and steaks. I haven't fired up the grill yet, so I'd better get to it. Needs to heat a while before I put the steaks on."

Paige started down the stairs but turned back. "When did you learn to cook? When you first got here, it was always me doing the cooking."

His smile was mixed parts amusement and guilt. "I always could cook a little. Besides, tonight is steak and potatoes. Any guy who can't throw potatoes in the oven, open a bag of salad and toss a couple of steaks on the grill should be required to turn in his manhood badge."

"Still, I appreciate the dinner. See you in a few."

She stripped off her clothes and jumped in the tub for a quick shower. Afterwards, she pulled on the satiny robe and tightened the silk belt about her waist, deciding to forgo any panties. The robe was cool against her heated flesh. The hem brushed the floor. When she walked, the material sinuously stroked her skin as her toes peeked out with each step. She loved it not only because Cash had given it to her but also because it fit her style and clothing tastes perfectly. Cash either knew her better than she'd realized or he'd been quite lucky in his selection.

The banging of the oven door alerted her to Cash's location. She headed to the kitchen and when there, struck a pose against the door frame, jutting one leg out the slit in the robe's front.

"What do you think?" she said.

Cash glanced over his shoulder and then back to

the potatoes he'd just pulled from the oven before looking again back to her.

"What I think is that dinner is going to be late."

He grabbed her hand and pulled her along up the stairs to his bedroom, with her laughing the entire way.

Dinner was late that night. Those were either the best steaks Paige had ever eaten, or the two hours in Cash's bedroom had worked up an appetite. She didn't know the answer to that question, but one question nagging her the rest of the night was when would her appetite for Cash diminish?

Through June, her appetite for Cash's touch never diminished. She was ravenous for him when she got home every evening. Fortunately, he seemed as starved as she, racing her to his bedroom, or hers, or to the shower, or the couch. Anywhere they could sate their hunger for each other.

In July, the small town of Whispering Springs began filling with tourists early in the week for the annual Fourth of July Arts and Crafts Festival. With the Fourth of July falling on a Friday, most visitors planned to stay through the weekend.

But like many Texas summers, July brought high temperatures and thick humidity. For Whispering Springs Medical Clinic, this meant an increase in emergency-room visits and new patients. By the Wednesday preceding the big county-sponsored fireworks display, the clinic had added fifteen new patients. This made the workdays fast-paced but long. When the clinic finally shut its doors for the day, Paige was ready to head home for a hot bath, a hot meal and an even hotter man.

On the Thursday before her three-day weekend, Paige's commute to work took ten minutes longer than usual due to the volume of traffic. She saw Marc Singer directing traffic near the clinic and got a smile and wave in return to her horn toot. Once she got parked, she raced into the office ready to apologize for her tardiness, but with this being Dr. Caroline Graham's first day back to work, the staff hadn't begun to work. They were all in the break room flipping through Caroline's album of pictures of her twins. However, once patients began filling the exam rooms, the day took off in its usual busy pace.

As the last patient was being seen, Paige remembered that in her haste that morning, she'd forgotten to crack open the windows on her car. With the day's heat, the interior would be unbearable.

"Lydia?"

"Hmm?" Lydia Henson continued entering her patient note in the computer.

"I need to run out and crack the windows on my car to let out some of the heat."

"Sure. No problem."

Paige slipped out the back door and headed for her car. There was no reason to physically get in the car since all she had to do was lean in, shove in her key to give power to the windows and then punch the buttons on the driver's door. She was leaning in when she felt something press into her back.

"Don't scream," a quaking male voice said. "Stand

up slowly. Don't make a scene and nobody will get hurt."

Paige slowly backed out of her car, fully aware of the gun shoved against her spine. "What do you want?" Her heart was racing. The sudden adrenaline surge in her bloodstream had the muscles all over her body jerking.

"Just do what I say and I won't hurt you."

Paige dug through her memory for some of her psychology training, but her brain was locked in fight-or-flight mode. And since she couldn't fight and flight wasn't an option, her mind couldn't give her any suggested action other than to do what the man said.

"What do you want?" she repeated in as calm a tone as possible. She risked a glance at the man. Dilated eyes. Dirty clothes. Acne-marked face. And she knew. Drugs. He wasn't going to rape her. He wanted drugs.

"I want you to let me in that back door you just came out of. That's it. Simple. Do that and nobody dies."

Paige shook her head. "I can't."

The man's face flamed red with rage. He slapped her with his left hand. Her head jerked backwards from the force of the blow. The right side of her head came alive in pain.

"Look, bitch. I told you what to do. I don't want to hurt you, but I will. I just need a little something to get me through the weekend. That's all. Now open the door."

He wasn't giving her any option. The lot they were

standing in was private and gated. No one could see them. No one would be coming to her rescue.

She prayed all the patients were gone. Most of the staff had taken off about thirty minutes ago, so only the two physicians and the receptionist should be in there. She must have thought too long because the next time he hit her, he used the butt of the gun. Pain shot through her head. When she touched her face, her fingers came back bloody. Her eyes watered from the pain.

"Are you stupid?" he shouted. "Open the fucking door."

He shoved her toward the locked rear door and its keypad. She punched in a code and pulled the handle. The door didn't open.

"Sorry. I'm nervous. I put in the wrong code. Let me do it again."

"Dumb bitch. Hurry up."

She punched in her five-digit code and the lock clicked. She pulled the door open. The man shoved her inside before she could take the first step on her own. She stumbled, hitting her shoulder on the wall.

"Now where's the drugs?"

"I don't have a key," Paige said. "They're locked up."

"Fuck!" he shouted. "Fuck, fuck, fuck. Get me the fucking key and get it right now."

"What's going on back here?"

Paige's heart sank when she heard Lydia Henson's voice.

"Nothing," Paige called back. "I just stumbled."

"Are you all right?" Lydia asked as she turned the corner. When she saw the man, the gun and probably the blood dripping down Paige's cheek, she froze.

"Are you a doctor?" the man said, waving his gun toward Lydia.

"I am. Are you hurt? Do you need a doctor?"

"Fuck, no, I don't need a doctor. I need me some oxy or Demerol. I know you've got some here."

"We don't keep strong narcotics in the office."

"Bullshit." His eyes were franticly sweeping around the hall. "Who else is here? Get them back here too." He waved the gun around and Paige feared he might accidentally shoot her or Lydia.

"Just us," Lydia said. "Everybody else is gone."

Lydia's voice was as soft and smooth as silk. Paige was impressed as hell that Lydia could sound so unaffected.

"Just Paige and me," she said again, a little louder. "Nobody else here."

"I'll tell you the same thing I told this stupid bitch here," he said, his waving gun almost hitting Paige in the face again. "Just give me the drugs and nobody gets hurt."

"Looks like my nurse has already gotten hurt," Lydia said.

"Naw. That's nothing. A little blood. But," he shoved the gun against Lydia's forehead, "if you don't get those keys out and give me those drugs, the next blood you're gonna see is your own."

Lydia nodded and pulled a set of keys from the pocket of her white coat. "Follow me."

She turned and began walking down the hall.

"Go on. You too," the man said as he shoved Paige in front of him.

Having a gun pointed at her back was surreal. Her mind knew it was happening, but a tiny sliver kept repeating, "Let me wake up."

But it was no dream. The reality that she could die, would never see Cash again, never again feel his hot, naked flesh pressed against her made her nauseous with fear. She wanted to live. She wasn't done living. Hell, she'd barely started living.

She followed Lydia into the examination rooms area and to a locked door. Once the door was open, Lydia stepped back with a wave of her hand, indicating the man should enter.

"No way, bitch. I'm not stupid."

Paige questioned that last statement in her mind.

"If I go in there, you'll try to shut the door." He put his hand on Lydia's back and pushed her inside. "Besides, you know where everything is. Get it. Put it in a sack or something."

Paige made a move to her left, hoping the drug addict would be so enamored by all the shelves of drugs, he might forget about her. Unfortunately, no. He roughly grabbed her arm and jerked her over to him. He put his arm around her neck, pressing her back to his front.

"Here's the deal, Doc." The man firmly pressed the cold end of the gun's barrel into Paige's temple. "You stop fucking around and get those drugs together and I won't have to kill your little nurse here. You keep delaying and she dies, then you die. Got it?"

For the first time, Paige saw the color leech from Lydia's face. "I understand. Don't do anything rash." She turned away and pulled a white plastic Walmart bag from the trash. "No reason for anyone to get hurt." She snapped the bag open and began raking bottles into the sack.

"Just the good stuff. I don't want no blood-pressure medicine or anything like that."

Lydia nodded and continued down the shelf. Once the bag was full, she turned and held it out to the druggie. "Here you go. Now let Paige go and get the hell out of my clinic."

Paige's heart was racing. His arm tightened against her throat. The man smelled like he hadn't showered in weeks. The stench of his body odor had been almost tolerable in an open parking lot, but inside this confined area the sour foulness was making her gag. Between his rancid smell and his forearm pressing on her trachea, she could barely draw a breath.

"Not so fast, Doc. Open that bag and show me what's in it."

Lydia shook the bag at him. "Take it and get out."

He tightened his arm on Paige's throat. Drawing a breath was like trying to suck a marble through a pinched straw. The lack of adequate oxygen had her seeing black spots. If he kept up that degree of restriction on her breathing, it was only a matter of time before she passed out.

Lydia opened the bag to display the contents. The man nodded.

"Good. Now follow me to the back door and I'll be gone."

He backed out of the room, dragging Paige with him, the gun still making its presence known against her temple.

"That's far enough," a male voice said. "Whispering Springs Sheriff's Department. Drop the gun and let the lady go."

Paige had never been so glad to hear Marc Singer's voice. The drug thief spun, dragging her along, putting her between him and the deputy's gun. Paige decided Marc had come in through the lobby door since he was between the man and the front exit.

"I don't think so," the druggie said. "This little lady and me are gonna walk out that back door. That way, nobody gets hurt. But if you don't do what I say, I might have to hurt this woman again."

Paige didn't think the gun could be pressed any more firmly into the side of her head than it was, but damned if the guy didn't indent her scalp a little more.

The sound of a shotgun being racked echoed through the empty hallway.

"When I was growing up, I used to be able to shoot the tail off a squirrel from quite a distance," Cash said. "At this distance, I figure shooting your brain out of your head will be a breeze."

Cash! Paige's heart leapt at the sound of his voice.

"Shit, Montgomery. I told you to stay outside," Marc said.

"And I'll be damned if I let you save my woman."

His woman? Paige's lack of adequate oxygen was playing mind games. That's what had to be going on.

"Well, don't splatter his brains yet," Marc said. "He might want to change his mind about going out the back door, seeing as how you're between him and that door."

Paige felt the man being jostled from behind.

"Come on, asshole. I already want to kill you for touching my woman. Just twitch. A little. You're about five seconds from being history."

Suddenly, Paige could draw a deep breath. The man's hands were in the air, the gun dangling off his index finger. Singer snatched the gun away. Using the butt of the shotgun, Cash bashed the guy upside his head.

"Hey. That guy hit me," the druggie said.

"Montgomery!" Singer said.

"Sorry. It slipped."

The corner of the deputy's mouth twitched. "Yeah, well, don't let it happen again." To the addict he said, "On the floor. Face down. Do it before I let Montgomery slip again."

The guy dropped to the floor, assumed the spread-eagle position. Cash kept his gun on him until Marc got the plastic cuffs on his prisoner. Even though the adrenaline was still flowing, the message didn't get to Paige's legs as they simply gave way and she collapsed to the floor. Lydia rushed over but she wasn't fast enough to be first. Cash dropped to his knees beside her.

He brushed the hair off her forehead. "Hey, honey. You okay?"

"Cash." She grabbed his hand. "You saved me."

"Naw. Singer had it under control." Still, when he wrapped her in his arms, she could feel them both shaking.

Caroline and Travis entered the room.

"Smart of you to enter the panic code," Caroline said. "When it rang at the front desk, Margie and I had time to hide. I think the sheriff's department was in the lobby within five minutes." She hugged Lydia and then stooped to hug Paige. "You are both so brave and quick thinking to stall him long enough for Marc to get in place." She stood. "Now, let's get you both in exam rooms and let me have a look."

Lydia shook her head. "I'm fine. A little shaken up and a whole lot mad, but physically only Paige needs attention."

Cash stood. "Do you want me to carry you to a room?"

Paige snorted, and then climbed to her feet with his support. "Don't be silly. I can walk."

But as she said the words, her knees gave out and she collapsed. Cash caught her and swung her up into his arms. "Where to, ladies?"

Paige's wounds were superficial. Small head cuts tended to bleed a lot and look more serious than they were, but Paige was still glad tomorrow was a holiday and she had three days off.

The Montgomery clan and Leo fussed over her the entire long weekend. Come Monday, she was thrilled to get back to work and her life back to normal. Not that all the caring wasn't nice, but she'd had almost no time alone with Cash, and she missed him.

Needless to say, their more-than-friends relationship was out in the open, and she had mixed feelings about that. On one hand, it was nice to be included in family nights with the Montgomerys and not worry about watching her every response to Cash. On the other hand, she felt a subtle pressure from the outside world—the Montgomerys and her brother—to make their romance more than it was.

And even though she and Cash didn't talk about it, she suspected he was feeling the same pressure and getting the same messages. But she didn't want to talk to him about it. It was the old rocking-the-boat idea. Everything was going great right now, why rock the boat?

The rest of July passed in a blur of busy days and nights in Cash's arms. She was as happy as she'd ever been.

The start of her graduate program was coming on fast, and while she hadn't changed her mind about going, she was questioning her upcoming move to Dallas. Maybe she could make the drive every day. Sure it'd make for some long days and late nights, but she'd be home with Cash every night.

And even though he hadn't said anything about love or marriage or the future, his tender touches said a lot. He'd begun to get serious about cooking, so dinner was always interesting, not always edible but interesting. But he did have steaks down to a fine art.

The work on the house had slowed through July. The end was in sight and Paige wondered if Cash was anxious about getting done with all his projects and having nothing to do. Not that he would ever tell her if that were true. Cash was the king of hiding feelings.

Chapter Twelve

For Cash, July was the month from hell, but with a life-changing twist. He'd almost lost Paige to a crazy druggie. That was the hell. But the twist?

When he'd seen her standing in the medical-clinic hallway, a man holding her tightly against him as a shield from Singer's gun, a feeling like none he'd ever experienced had swept over him. An emotion so strong and so stunning that it had almost dropped him to his knees. He loved Paige Ryan. Loved her with every ounce of his being.

And wasn't that a kick? In love with a woman who'd made it clear their summer fling was just that… a fling. An affair with a deadline, a deadline that was rushing toward them. He still wasn't good enough for her, but he wanted to be, even if it took the rest of his life to get there.

She'd said *fling*, but he was sure there was more

between them than that. He debated telling her how he felt, but part of loving her meant wanting her to achieve her dreams, and right now, that meant graduate school.

The last time love had been mentioned, he'd totally screwed up her life. He couldn't take the chance that a selfish declaration on his part could throw Paige off her plans. He could wait out the year she was in school. Wait until she was done and back in Whispering Springs and ready to settle down. She was still young. Hell, technically, so was he at twenty-nine. They had their whole lives ahead of them. Waiting a year or so to start that life together would be no big deal.

He liked the feeling of Paige next to him in bed. It felt natural, as if there was no time before them.

However, there were times when he worried that not telling her how much he loved her could screw up *his* life. Their summer was almost over. She'd put a deposit on an apartment in university housing. She'd begun talking about classes and homework and nerves about matching up with the others in the class.

Through all those conversations about the school and the next year and the work after graduation, she never said a word about them, their future. She gave him the impression that what they had was here and now.

And that worried him…a lot.

By early August, renovations were mostly completed on the house. Since the Singing Springs ranch house already had four bedrooms, converting the old bedroom at the back of the house into a large master suite seemed to be a waste of Travis's money.

Instead, Cash used some of his rodeo winnings to rebuild the space into an exercise room with a large whirlpool tub and sauna. Travis told Cash that he was nuts to put that kind of money into the old house, but Cash was growing fond of the place. The more time he spent there, the more it felt like home, and for a man who hadn't had a permanent home in eleven years, it was a feeling he liked. Plus, he was enjoying the physical labor involved in rebuilding this house board-by-board.

He was finishing some touch-up paint around the windows when he heard a knock at the back door. After cleaning his hands, he found Rusty Webster, the oldest son of Travis's foreman, at the door.

"Hi, Rusty. What can I do for you?"

He shoved an envelope at Cash. "I was supposed to bring this over last night and I forgot. Don't tell Dad or Mr. Montgomery, okay?"

The return address on the envelope was Halo M Ranch. Travis had said he was sending a check for some supplies. Cash stuck the envelope in his back pocket.

"It's our secret, kid. Thanks for bringing it over."

"Thanks, Cash." Rusty looked over his shoulder. "Gotta run before I get caught. Supposed to be exercising Willard."

The teen rushed toward an aging gelding who was more interested in eating the grass than walking. Rusty climbed on and, after quite a bit of prodding, got the old guy moving back toward Halo M.

Cash shut the door with a smile. That boy stayed with one foot in trouble and the other on a wet bar of soap.

Travis's timing was perfect. Cash was going to the bank this afternoon anyway, so he'd throw this check into his account. After sliding his finger under the flap, he pulled out the check and froze. He held his breath as he studied the check made out to Paige Ryan for one thousand dollars. For a moment, his vision swam making him nauseous.

Why would his brother be giving Paige a thousand dollars?

In the memo area was the notation *Thank you.* What the hell did that mean? Thank you? What was Travis thanking her for?

His first reaction was to call Travis and demand an explanation. But instead of getting a straight answer, Travis would be all over the fact Cash had opened Paige's mail instead of the real issue, which was…why in the hell was he paying Paige a thousand dollars?

Cash paced and thought. Was Paige being paid to house-sit this old place? That didn't make any sense either since she'd started out paying rent.

Had she bought something and Travis was reimbursing her? That didn't seem logical.

The next thought made his stomach heave gastric acid into his throat. Was Paige being paid to watch him? Had his brother sunk so low as to pay a woman to sleep with him, take care of him? He swallowed against the rising knot in his throat. The whole idea made him sick.

He glanced at the clock on the stove. Paige should be home in less than an hour. He'd have his answers then.

THE END OF THE WORK DAY COULDN'T COME FAST enough for Paige. Last night, Cash had finished caulking in the new two-person whirlpool, and tonight they were going to break it in. Cash could be so inventive when it came to sex. Her heart skipped at the thought of being in all the swirling water with him and his ideas.

She vibrated with nervous energy all day. Her mood had been so upbeat and spunky that Mr. Francis had asked her if she'd had too much caffeine.

With a ton of resolve, she kept the distressing reality that the end of summer was just around the corner from overwhelming her. No matter that the separation would hurt, no matter where her life took her, this summer would always remain in her memories as *the* summer of her life.

Over the years, she'd learned a lot about herself, such as there was nothing she couldn't do if she put her mind to it, except maybe one thing. She couldn't make herself fall out of love with Cash, not that the word *love* had ever come up between them.

Seven years ago, he'd walked out when she'd told him that she loved him. She promised herself that this time, she'd keep that little tidbit to herself, and she had. It was hard, but she'd done it. She wouldn't hold her breath that he'd ask her to stay or confess his undying love or tell her he couldn't live without her. She wasn't a child. It was time to put away childish fantasies such as those. He'd given her exactly what she'd asked for…commitment-free sex.

She patted the two bottles of sparkling grape juice beside her. Now they would celebrate the new construction and the end of the summer. Champagne would have been nice, but really, she didn't need the alcohol. Just a naked Cash in a swirling pool of hot water.

She whipped her car into the drive. Gravel spewed behind her tires. She brought the car to a skidding stop in front and then slammed the gears into park. She grabbed the two bottles of juice and hopped out, ready to christen the tub properly.

To her surprise, Cash was sitting in the downstairs living room when she walked in the door. He didn't wear the expression of a man about to get very, *very* lucky. Instead, the phrase *dead man walking* came to mind.

"Cash. What's wrong?" She sat the bottles on the coffee table. "You look like your best friend just died."

He held out a piece of paper. She recognized the check from the Halo M account. She didn't take it.

"Why is my brother paying you a thousand dollars?"

"That's between Travis and me." She knew he'd never let that answer stand, but she was frantically searching her mind for what to say. Unfortunately, her mind had shut down.

"Did you buy something for Caroline and he's paying you back?"

He'd given her the perfect out. She should take it.

But she couldn't.

"No."

"Then explain this money."

"I don't have to explain anything to you. It's really none of your business. You'll just have to trust me."

Cash stood and the air was sucked from the room. Her knees wobbled in her pink scrub pants. Her heart wobbled in her chest. He put both hands on her shoulders and held her until she met his dark gaze.

"Is my brother paying you to watch me? Are you my hired live-in nurse?"

She tried to speak but there were no words. Nothing she could say would make this better. Lying was not one of her strengths, so that wasn't an option. She swallowed against the boulder lodged in her throat.

He gave her the slightest of shakes. "Are you being paid by my brother to watch me? Report back to him?" He let out a snort of derision. "I hope you asked for more money once you had to start fucking me. I'm sure that wasn't part of the agreement."

Paige slapped him. "How insulting."

"Insulting?" He shoved off and walked away a few steps before turning to face her. "Insulting is finding out that my brother is paying you to spy on me."

"I never said—"

"You never denied it either."

Paige's legs gave way and she collapsed on the sofa. "It wasn't like that. He didn't pay me to spy on you."

"Then explain this." He waved the check in her direction.

She blew out a long sigh. "He just wanted to make sure you were okay. Had food in the house. Had what you needed. But not spy on you. Never spy on you."

Cash raked his hands through his short hair. "Fuck a duck. He couldn't care less about this house, could he? All the money he spent to fix it up was just to keep my hands busy and me out of Leo's. Am I right?" He banged his open hand on a doorframe. "Am I right?"

"I don't know, Cash. I really don't."

"Fuck!" He hit the doorframe again and then his head sagged. "Why did you take it? The money. Why?"

"At first, I was still a little mad from our run-in that morning. Then—" she shrugged, "—I thought why not? I was going to let you stay here anyway and then Travis offered to help pay for my graduate program if I would…."

"Would what? Give him reports? Tell him if I was drinking? In case you and my nosey family hadn't noticed, I haven't been."

"I noticed, Cash. I noticed a lot of things. How much stronger you've gotten. How you barely limp now. How tan your face has become. How much you laugh these days."

"And of course you reported all this to my family."

"No. I told you, I didn't spy. Travis loves you. Your family adores you. Travis just wanted to make sure you had what you needed." She pushed off the couch and walked over to him. When she touched his shoulder, he shrugged her off. Her heart sank.

"Don't. Just don't touch me right now."

"I'm sorry, Cash. When I agreed to make sure you had food and a roof over your head, I didn't know we would…" She couldn't say fall in love because she was the only one in that boat. "Get so close," she finished.

He snorted. "Close? Not hardly. We are about as far apart as two people can be." He headed toward the kitchen and the back of the house.

"Where are you going? Cash?" She hurried after him and caught him at the back door.

"I don't know, but don't worry. Your job here is done. I'll be back after you've moved out." The look he gave her broke her heart. His expression was etched with hurt and pain. The fire in his eyes was gone, replaced by a flat stare. "You always were going to leave. I kept forgetting that. Maybe now is as good a time as any. When you've got your things out, let Travis know. He'll let me know. Leave your key on the kitchen table."

"I'm not through talking." Her voice shook. Not so much with anger at his reaction, but with regret and sadness that he was walking out on her again.

"I am." He opened the door. "We could have had a chance," he said without turning around. "I really cared about you. I was just fooling myself. I can't trust you. And apparently, you have so little trust in me that you kept this secret for months. Have a nice life, Paige."

She watched through the back door window as Cash climbed into his truck, started it and drove out of her life.

She wanted to run after him, tell him that she loved him, but he'd never believe that. Not now.

The new place was ready. She could move in any time. The deposit was paid. The small apartment had furniture. All it needed was her clothes and Ruby's litter box and she'd be moved in.

She'd gone into this relationship—or whatever it was—with no promises and an understanding that when she left, it was over. So maybe her leaving had come a little sooner than she'd expected. She could pack and be out of here within the hour. Let him come home to an empty house. That'd teach him a lesson.

She dropped into a chair. Stubborn jackass. If he'd waited around for another minute, she'd have told him that she'd returned every check Travis had sent and would return this one too. But no. He had to storm out of the house like a warrior going to battle.

Seven years ago, she'd let him walk out of her trailer and out of her life. However, she wasn't the same woman today that she'd been then. She was willing to fight for what she wanted.

He wasn't going to get the last word this time. He wasn't going to run her off, and she wasn't going to let him storm off without an explanation. He'd listen to what she had to say if she had to tie him in a chair.

And it was past time for him to do a little explaining himself, even if his explanation was seven years overdue.

If it's a battle he wants, a battle he'd get. Bring it on.

Chapter Thirteen

Cash drove around for almost an hour, fighting with himself. He didn't just *care* about Paige, he loved her. So maybe he hadn't said it, but she had to know.

And maybe he shouldn't have walked out, but the fact that the woman he loved had sided with his family to spy on him hurt more than any damage Bad Bob or any bull had inflicted on him. A future with a woman he didn't trust was out of the question.

Damn it! He slammed his fist on the truck's steering wheel.

There was another person to blame besides Paige.

He did a U-turn and headed back toward Singing Springs, except he turned into the Halo M drive instead. He floored it down the drive and jammed on his brakes on at Travis's front porch. Travis and Jason were sitting in rockers as though expecting him.

Cash climbed out of the truck and slammed the

door with a loud thud. Travis set his iced tea on the table and rose.

"Hello, Cash."

"Don't you hello me, you sonofabitch."

Travis walked down the stairs and stood in front of Cash. But before Travis could say a word, Cash let a right fist fly, which caught Travis on the chin. His head rocked back from the blow.

Cash's knuckles screamed in pain after the hit. Damn man had a jaw of steel.

Travis's eyes narrowed. "I'll let you have that one, little brother, because I know you're upset. But—" His next words were lost in an *oomph* as Cash landed a solid fist in Travis's gut. Travis doubled over from the strike and then straightened.

Cash danced around on his toes, his fists poised for another blow. But his older brother had always been faster and stronger. Travis's first hit split Cash's lower lip. Cash's response landed on Travis's shoulder.

The two men exchanged blows but no words, for a couple of minutes. Finally, Travis landed a powerful punch under Cash's chin that sent him reeling backwards and then to the ground.

Travis stood over him, his fists still bunched.

From the porch, Jason clapped and whistled. "Best fight in ages, boys."

Cash looked over at Jason and wheezed out, "Fuck you," which made Jason laugh and clap louder.

Caroline stood alongside Jason, her hands on her hips, displeasure etched on her face.

Travis held out his hand, his breath coming in great heaving gasps. "We done?"

Cash considered grabbing that hand and jerking his brother down for a few more rounds, but in the end, he nodded. "Done fightin', but not done cussing you out." Cash took satisfaction that his older brother was panting as hard as he was.

Travis nodded. "I'm okay with that."

Cash took the offered hand and his brother pulled him to his feet.

"You were expecting me?" Cash said, supporting himself with his hands braced on his thighs.

"Paige called. Your woman has quite the vocabulary when she's mad."

Cash straightened and then wiped the blood from his lip. "She's not *my woman*, thanks to you."

Travis swiped at the blood oozing from the cut over his left eye. "Not my fault you're such as ass that you didn't stay around to listen to what Paige was trying to tell you."

"You *paid* her to live with me," Cash shouted. "How can she explain that away?"

Caroline walked up, wet cloth in hand. "Stand still. Let me see if either of you needs stitches."

Cash gritted his teeth as Caroline wiped the blood from his face. "I don't need stitches. I want to kill your husband for ruining my life."

"You did that pretty much on your own," Jason tossed down from the porch, which got him a one-finger salute from Cash.

Travis climbed the steps to the porch and picked

up a stack of envelopes off a table. "If you'd hung around your house instead of racing over here to tear off my head, *your woman* would have told you she returned every check." He waved the white stack at Cash. "Every single check. Not one cashed, even though she could have used the money for school."

Cash's heart skipped a beat. "What?"

Caroline put her arm around Cash. "He meant well, Cash. He really did." She gave him a one-armed hug. "He was worried about you. Didn't want you to leave town because you had no place to live. Some of this is my fault. I'm the one who told Paige she could have my uncle's place."

Cash looked at his sister-in-law. "You bear no fault at all. He wrote the checks. He's the one who meddled in my life."

"Don't you see, Cash?" Caroline asked. "Paige returned Travis's money because she cares about you. She wants to be with you. She wasn't with you because it was expected or paid for. It was because it was her way of loving you."

"I suspect that check you opened would have been on its way back to me by now."

"But why did you keep sending money when she kept sending them back?"

Travis's face flushed. "Okay, maybe I was meddling a little. As long as she sent them back, I knew things were good over there. The minute she cashed one, I would know there were problems." He shrugged. "I was wrong. I admit it. But damn, little brother, I didn't want to lose you again into a bottle or have you leave town."

Travis dropped the returned checks on the table and jumped over the railing into the yard. "You were gone too long, Cash. You're home and we all want you to stay."

Jason followed Travis over the railing. "Yeah, bro. I didn't know about the checks, but if I had, I would have told you." He glared at Travis. "Damn, stupid thing to do." He looked at Cash. "But his heart was in the right place."

Cash looked at Travis. "His heart might have been in the right place but his head was up his ass."

Before Travis could respond, large balls of hail began pounding down on top of them.

"What the…?" Cash said, looking up.

"Oh hell," Travis said. "Look at the sky."

What had been a late afternoon orange sky was now a dark green. Around them, the wind was picking up. From nowhere, pieces of paper began flying around the yard.

Travis grabbed Caroline's arm. "Looks bad. We need to get to safety." They bounded up the stairs, Jason and Cash close on their heels. They paused on the porch to study the weather.

"Where are the kids?" Jason asked.

"At Mom's. I'll call her and—"

"Oh crap. Look," Jason said, pointing to a dark swirling cloud.

"What?" Cash said. "I can't hear you."

The sound bearing down on them was almost deafening. The swirling cloud took shape. Large, cylindrical and dark, a funnel touched in a field about a mile away. Dirt lifted into the vortex. Trees and shrubs were ripped from the ground like weeds and tossed aside.

"Tornado," Travis yelled. "Inside."

But nobody moved. The black whirlpool turned away from Halo M and Travis's house and took direct aim for Singing Springs Ranch.

"Paige!" Cash shouted. "She's there."

Jason grabbed his arm. "Maybe it'll pass the house. You can't go right now. You'll be killed."

Even though the house was just shy of a mile away, their field of vision was unimpeded. First, shingles lifted, and then they were ripped from the roof and added to the trash circling in the air. Then boards and windows followed. Jerked off and thrown into the surrounding fields.

Cash vibrated with fear and the need to do something, but from this distance, there was nothing he could do but stand by helplessly and watch as the house he'd rebuilt was destroyed board by board, with the woman he loved trapped in the destruction.

Gleaming-white exterior boards, glass and roof shingles flew in the air and littered the fields around the now demolished house. Torrential rain poured from the black storm clouds. As quickly as it came, the tornado lifted off the ground and disappeared back into the dark sky.

Cash jerked his arm out of Jason's grasp and raced to his truck.

"Cash," Travis called. "Wait."

He waved off his brother's order, threw himself into his truck and whipped the vehicle around in a U-turn, leaving deep ruts in the front yard. The distance between the two ranches was less than a mile, but it felt like it took an hour to cover the short distance. After turning into what was left of Singing Springs's entry gate, Cash had to maneuver his truck over downed trees, electric wires and all manner of trash and debris to get to the site of the devastated house.

His breath left his lungs in a whoosh. There wasn't a wall left standing. Furniture, clothes and books were scattered in the mud. That was all unimportant. The only thing that he cared about was where was Paige?

The wind had picked up again, howling through what trees still had limbs and leaves. The rain beat down, driving into his flesh like sharp needles. It didn't matter. Nothing mattered if Paige was dead.

Looking over the destruction, his heart sank. Nothing could be alive under all those heavy boards.

"Paige! Can you hear me?" He couldn't hear anything but the slamming of his own heart. "Paige!" Lifting a board off the pile, he chucked it off into the yard.

He startled when a hand grabbed his shoulder. He whirled. Travis and Jason were standing there. Behind them, Caroline was climbing out of the Halo M work truck.

"Where do you want us to go?" Travis asked, pulling on his work gloves.

Shaking off his surprise, Cash pointed toward the

kitchen, or rather where the kitchen had been. Travis and Jason began working through the rubble while Cash made his way around to where Paige's bedroom had been. The complete and total devastation of the building was like nothing he'd ever seen. There was no way Paige was in this area of the house. Simply put, there was nothing left.

"Paige," he called. "Buster. Here, boy." He thought maybe the dog might be capable of hearing better than a human.

He had to keep thinking she was alive and just couldn't hear him. While he'd once believed he'd understood what Travis had felt when his wife died, now he realized he hadn't had a clue. If Paige was dead…he wouldn't let himself think that way.

"Buster. Come here, boy. Buster." He continued calling as he made his way around the side of the house.

"Cash. Come here." Jason's voice was barely audible from the backyard.

Cash hurried back around, slipping and sliding in the mud. "What? Did you find her?"

"Hush. Listen."

The four adults stood straining to hear any sound of life.

"I don't hear anything," Cash said.

"Call Buster again," Jason said. "I could have sworn I heard a dog."

Cash began calling and walking toward the side of the house opposite Paige's bedroom, and then he began running. "Back here, guys. I hear Buster's bark."

His brothers hurried to catch up with him.

"The storm cellar," Travis said. "I forgot all about it."

"What storm cellar?" Jason asked.

"Later." Cash reached the underground door. "Paige. Are you in there?"

The reply was muffled but it came.

Cash dropped to his knees, wet mud saturating through his jeans. "Thank you, God. Thank you."

This was not the time to tell her that he loved her. He couldn't just yell it through a storm door. Still, the relief at hearing her voice made him more sure than ever that this was *his* woman, the one he would spend the rest of his life with, and he'd do whatever it took to convince her of that.

"We're coming, honey. Can you hear me? Hold on. I'm coming for you."

There was a muffled response, but the words were lost through the metal and rain.

"Are you hurt?" Cash shouted. "Can you bang on the door? Once if you're okay."

The response was the dampened sound of something hitting the door once. She was okay. She would be okay.

Adrenaline raced through his veins. He was sure he could rip away all the piles of limbs and house wreckage covering the metal door barehanded. However, that wasn't the problem. The hurdle was the hundred-year-old oak lying across the door. Cash began pushing on the trunk of a tree his arms couldn't have circled.

"Hold on, babe." He grunted as he shoved at the tree. "I love you. Hold on." The words were out of his mouth before he knew it, but they were honest and exactly what he was feeling. He'd almost lost the opportunity to tell her. To hell with it. He'd be telling her that every day for years to come.

"Cash," Travis called. "You'll never move that alone. Move over."

Cash was joined by both his brothers, and all three of them pulled together to move the impossible.

"Caroline. Back my truck up as close as you can get," Cash said. "Travis. You got any rope in your truck? We can try to pull the tree off the door or at least dislodge it enough to get her out."

Travis nodded and headed off with his wife to position Cash's truck and get the strong rope he always had in the truck bed. More than once he'd needed rope to get a horse or a cow out of trouble.

"Thanks, man," Cash said to Jason.

"For what?"

"For coming over to help."

"God, Cash. You are a damn fool. You're my brother. Of course I'd come help. We're family. We've always been here for you. You just never asked."

Cash realized how right Jason was. He hadn't asked his family for help. He'd spent his life trying to prove himself to them, except they'd never asked him to do that. Of course his siblings had pushed and teased and dared him when he was growing up, but he finally understood that he was the only one who thought they didn't believe him good enough. He was the one with the problem, not them.

"Yeah, well, I should have."

The roar of Cash's diesel engine cut through the sound of rain as Caroline backed it in close to the tree. Travis returned with a chainsaw, took off a few of the larger limbs that might impede movement and then made a notch in the tree trunk for the rope. After they got the rope in place around the tree and secured it to the truck, Caroline eased forward while the three men pushed at the tree to roll it off the door enough to get it open.

As soon as the last inch of tree trunk slid off, Cash went to work on the doors.

"Paige. Honey. Can you hear me? Have you unbolted the door?"

An unintelligible response came back.

Cash tugged on the door handle but nothing budged.

"Help me," he said to his brothers, who took up positions on either side. Together they pulled the warped doors upward.

And then he saw her face. Her smile. Her beautiful eyes. His Paige.

She handed out a small bag with Ruby stuffed inside. The kitten's indignant howls conveyed the horror of her situation.

Then Buster was handed up. He greeted the Montgomery men with yaps and puppy kisses, excited to have attention.

Finally, Paige climbed the ladder. Sheer elation rolled through Cash when her head popped through the small opening. Reaching down, he grabbed under her arms and pulled her out. Then he immediately wrapped her in his arms and began kissing her. Her forehead. Her cheeks. Her lips.

"Oh my God," he said, a definite choke to his voice. "I thought I'd lost you forever. I love you, Paige. Love you, love you, love you."

"I love you too. I've loved you my whole life."

"I hate to break this up," Jason said with a slap on Cash's back. "But I'm wet and cold and starving. Think we can head back to Halo M now?"

Cash took one last nibble of Paige's lips before he looked at his family. "I love you guys. I'll never be able to repay you."

Travis laughed. "Don't worry. I'm sure we'll think of something."

Caroline slid her arm around her husband's waist. "Jason's right. Let's get home so I can see if any of you need medical attention."

"I don't, but we need to check on Mom and Dad and the kids," Travis said. "I want to make sure the storm didn't do any damage over there."

"Lydia too," Jason said as he started jogging toward the truck.

Cash wanted that in his life. A woman he loved who loved him back. And he'd finally found her.

WHEN THEY GOT BACK TO HALO M, JACKIE AND

Lane Montgomery were waiting in the kitchen. The twins had been at their house during the storm, and when Jackie couldn't get an answer at Halo M, they'd loaded up the kids and headed over.

"Hi, Mom," Cash said, his arm still firmly wrapped about Paige's shoulder.

Jackie stood and hugged Cash and Paige. "I am so sorry, honey. Your father and I saw what's left of your house when we got here."

"It's just a house." Cash squeezed Paige. "I got the most important thing out of there."

"Thanks, Jackie," Paige said. "I've never been through anything like that in my life."

Jackie pulled Paige over to a chair. "I'm so glad you are okay." She eyed Paige's clothes.

"What are you wearing?"

Paige looked down and smiled. She was dressed in the robe Cash had given her and had his silver buckle belt wrapped twice around her waist. "I only had two minutes warning to get to shelter. I was wearing this at the time. I grabbed Ruby, shoved her in my purse, snatched up Buster and raced for the storm shelter. If Cash hadn't put in the new door on that side of the house, I don't think I would have made it."

Cash stood behind her chair, water dripping from his hair and clothes. He threaded his fingers into Paige's hair. "Thank God, I did that." He leaned over and kissed her in front of his entire family. "I don't want to think about the alternative."

"Enough," Caroline announced. "We are all soaked to the skin. Showers and dry clothes for everybody. Paige, there's clean towels and whatever you'll need in the guest bath upstairs. I'll find you something to put on. Cash, you can use Noah's bath, but no promises what condition it's in."

Paige rose. "Thanks, Caroline. Hospital scrubs will be fine."

Travis headed to the master suite while Jason bided his turn for the showers by drying the best he could with a towel. Cash's gaze never left Paige as she exited the kitchen and headed up the stairs.

"Go on," Jackie said on a sigh. "I'll pretend I'm not your mother."

Cash laid a quick kiss on his mother's cheek and raced after Paige.

PAIGE WAS JUST STEPPING INTO THE SHOWER WHEN the door burst open and a panting Cash stepped into the bathroom.

"I thought it would be considerate if we showered together. You know, to save water." The twinkle in his eyes said he was thinking about anything but water conservation, but damned if she'd argue.

Okay, she giggled a little as he rocked from side-to-side and bounced off the wall a couple of times struggling to get wet denim down his legs. But the thick material would only slide down an inch at a time.

"Stop laughing," he snarled, but there was no heat behind the words.

He stripped off the rest of his clothes and then pushed her under the shower spray. Hot water rolled down her back and she wasn't sure if it was that or the hot male flesh pressing into her front that was sending ripples of delight through her.

She nibbled on his neck. "I think I heard something about love." Pulling back, she stared into his crystal-blue eyes. "Was that just the heat of the moment speaking? I understand if it was, and I'll be okay if you tell me it was," she lied. "But it won't change how I feel about you. Ever. I love you, Cash. I know that scares you. Makes you want to run away, but it's too much to hold in any longer. I love you."

He grinned and kissed her. "The only heat of the moment was blurting it out in front of my brothers instead of in front of you." Pulling her snug against him, he trapped his engorged shaft between then. "I do love you, Paige. I was going to tell you, just not like that. I want you to go to school and get that degree. I won't let my feelings interrupt your future."

"You're an idiot," she said with a laugh. "Loving you won't interrupt my future. It makes my future." She took his mouth in a deep kiss, thrusting her tongue between his lips, seeking to lock the taste of him in her mind. She felt him flinch. "What's wrong?"

He rubbed at a cut on his lip. "Still a little tender."

"Poor baby. What happened?"

"Long story, but let's just say that Travis and I had a discussion about his meddling in my life."

She laughed and went back in for a kiss, but making sure to move her lips gently on that side.

THEIR SHOWER TOOK LONGER THAN SHE'D PLANNED but when the cool water sluiced down her hair and back, she turned off the dial and pushed Cash out. "We used all the hot water. Your family will be taking cold showers because of us."

Cash snatched a fluffy white towel off the counter and began rubbing her abdomen. "I'll apologize." The grin he gave her was saucy and totally unapologetic. "But I'm not sorry."

Paige pulled the towel away. "Get dressed before they send someone up here to see why we've been gone so long."

After a kiss he said, "Yeah, like they don't know."

TWO WEEKS LATER, CASH PULLED HIS TRUCK DOWN his parents' drive at Bar M Ranch. Beside him, Paige held two wrapped presents.

"You think Caroline and Travis realized their wedding day was so close to Adam's birthday?" Paige asked.

"I doubt it. From what I understand from Travis about their wedding, it wasn't a planned date as much as it was the only day they had with Caroline's grandmother." He pulled the truck behind Drake Gentry's Range Rover. "I can't believe they've been married a year." He shook his head. "Where did the year go?"

"I'm just pleased at how happy they are." She pointed to a small boy with a dog. "How old is Adam today?"

"Seven." He cleared his throat. "Um, you might

be warned that his mother might be a little upset with me, Travis and Jason."

She rolled her eyes toward him. "What have y'all done?"

"You'll see." He grinned. "C'mon. Let's join the anniversary slash birthday party."

Adam looked toward them when the truck doors slammed. A smile as wide as his face split his mouth and he ran toward them.

"Thank you, Uncle Cash. Thank you. I've always wanted a horse."

Olivia Landry followed her son to where they stood. "Hi, Paige." She looked at Cash. "You, I'm not speaking to." But the sparkle in her eyes gave away her mirth.

"Oh, sis. You know you love me." Cash pulled her into his arms, gave her a loud smacking kiss on her cheek and then messed up her hair.

Paige brushed a kiss on Olivia's cheek. "A horse?"

"Oh, yes. After I distinctly told my brothers not to buy a horse for Adam for his birthday, that arrived this morning." She pointed to a chestnut-brown colt. "Meet Rocky."

Paige chuckled. "He's lovely."

"He'll grow up with me," Adam said. "I'll love him forever."

Cash knew his sister would forgive them. Every little boy had to have his own horse, at least in his family they did.

"And how old were you when you got your first horse, sis?"

Olivia flipped her hair over her shoulder. "Irrelevant."

"How old were you, Momma?" Adam asked.

Cash leaned over to his nephew. "She was seven."

Adam laughed. "The same age as me."

"Now that your uncle Cash and Paige are here, let's go cut the cake," Olivia said, clearly redirecting her son. Over her shoulder, she whispered, "If you two ever have a son, I'm buying him a set of drums. Two can play at this game." She followed Adam as he raced toward the house.

Paige slipped her arm around Cash's waist. "Oops. You might have won this battle, but I think the real war is ahead."

Cash slung his arm around her shoulders. "Gotta love a good family scrimmage that'll take years to win."

Walking with Paige, their arms intertwined, Cash knew his plans for the day were right. He belonged with Paige and she belonged with him. Forever.

Wedding anniversary presents for Travis and Caroline had to wait until Adam tore through his stack of birthday presents. Boots. Gloves. A new saddle—from his dad who'd known about the horse. A hat. And more toys and books than Cash could count.

Unlike Adam, who ripped and tore his way through his gifts, Caroline was much more restrained as she opened the few anniversary gifts for Travis and her. Each gift was pronounced as perfect before being handed off to one of the other women to see.

The men stood off to the side, each of them with a drink in hand. Beer for some. Soft drinks for others.

"You're a lucky man," Cash said to Travis with a tip of his glass of Coke toward Caroline.

"Don't I know it," Travis said with a smile. "I don't deserve her, but whatever you do, don't tell her."

Cash laughed.

"So, little bro, when you stepping up to the plate?" Jason asked.

Cash frowned. "That's an excellent question." He looked over at the women in his family sitting on his parents' patio. The men were gathered with him. Adam was over in the pasture running with his new colt. "You know what they say. No time like the present."

He stepped away and walked over to the women. Their high-toned voices quieted when he knelt beside Paige's chair. She turned toward him.

"What's wrong, Cash?"

He pulled a small black velvet box from his front pants pocket. "What's wrong is your last name. I want to change it to Montgomery." He popped open the box and the two-carat oval-diamond engagement ring sparkled in the late afternoon sun. "Will you marry me?"

Paige's mouth dropped. Tears began filling her eyes.

Behind him, he heard the shuffle of boot soles as the men in his family joined the women on the patio. No one spoke as they waited for her answer.

Her hand went to her mouth. Her gaze shot from him, to the ring, and back to him.

"Ohmigod. Ohmigod. Are you serious?"

Cash smiled. "I'm serious. Marry me. Hell, you need to make an honest man out of me. You've made me live in sin with you for months."

She laughed and threw her arms around his neck. "Of course I'll marry you. I love you." She covered his face with kisses.

Around them, his family cheered and applauded. It didn't matter what twists and turns life held for them. As long as they were together, they could weather any storm.

Photo by Tom Smarch

New York Times and USA Today Bestselling Author Cynthia D'Alba was born and raised in a small Arkansas town. After being gone for a number of years, she's thrilled to be making her home back in Arkansas living on the banks of an eight-thousand acre lake.

When she's not reading or writing or plotting, she's doorman for her spoiled border collie, cook, housekeeper and chief bottle washer for her husband and slave to a noisy, messy parrot. She loves to chat online with friends and fans.

Send snail mail to: Cynthia D'Alba PO Box 2116 Hot Springs, AR 71914

Or better yet! She would for you to take her newsletter. She promises not to spam you, not to fill your inbox with advertising, and not to sell your name and email address to anyone. Check her website for a link to her newsletter.

www.cynthiadalba.com
cynthiadalba@gmail.com

Read on for more
Whispering Springs, Texas books
by
Cynthia D'Alba

TEXAS TWO STEP

WHISPERING SPRINGS, TEXAS BOOK 1 ©2012
CYNTHIA D'ALBA

Secrets are little time-bombs just waiting to explode.

After six years and too much self-recrimination, rancher Mitch Landry admits he was wrong. He left Olivia Montgomery. Now he'll do whatever it take to convince Olivia to give him a second chance.

Olivia Montgomery survived the break-up with the love of her life. She's rebuilt her life around her business and the son she loves more than life itself. She's not proud of the mistakes she's made—particularly the secret she's kept—but when life serves up manure, you use it to mold yourself into something better.

At a hot, muggy Dallas wedding, they reconnect, and now she's left trying to protect the secret she's held on to for all these years.

Read on for an excerpt:

The woman stood on tiptoe in the baggage-claim area of the Dallas/Fort Worth airport looking for all the world like someone who'd been sent to collect the devil. Mitch Landry had expected Wes or one of the other groomsmen to come for him. Instead, his gaze found a statuesque blonde arching up on her toes, a white T-shirt with Jim's Gym in black script stretched across her lushly curved breasts and long tanned legs extending from tight denim shorts. His heart stumbled then roared into a gallop.

Blood rushed from his brain to below his waist. His nostrils flared in a deep breath, as though he could smell her unique fragrance across the crowded lobby.

She hadn't looked in his direction yet, which gave him an unfettered opportunity to study her without having to camouflage his reactions.

No make-up covered her creamy rose complexion, not that she needed any. Not then and not now. No eye shadow was required to bring out the deep blue of her eyes. Nor did her mouth need any enhancement. Her lips radiated a natural pink, although the bottom one grew redder as her upper teeth gnawed on it.

Six years had passed since he'd seen Olivia Montgomery, but he'd swear she was more beautiful today. She had an appeal that came only with age and maturity. A smile edged onto his mouth. He was surprised —pleasantly surprised—to admit how glad he was to see her.

He watched as her glare bounced around the room, searching faces until it fell on him. As a look of resignation flashed across her face, she frowned.

His smile faded. Not exactly the reaction he'd hoped for.

TEXAS TANGO

WHISPERING SPRINGS,TEXAS, BOOK 2 © 2013
CYNTHIA D'ALBA

Sex in a faux marriage can make things oh so real.

Dr. Caroline Graham is happy with her nomadic lifestyle fulfilling short-term medical contracts. No emotional commitments, no disappointments. She's always the one to walk away, never the one left behind. But now her grandmother is on her deathbed, more concerned about Caroline's lack of a husband than her own demise. What's the harm in a little white lie? If a wedding will give her grandmother peace, then a wedding she shall have.

Widower Travis Montgomery devotes his days to building the ranch he and his late wife planned before he lost her to breast cancer. The last piece of acreage he needs is controlled by a lady with a pesky need of her own. Do her a favor and he can have the land. She needs a quick, temporary, faux marriage in exchange for the acreage.

It's a total win-win situation until events begin to snowball and they find, instead of playacting, they've put their hearts at risk.

Read on for an excerpt:

Friday afternoon, Travis Montgomery pulled his truck under the only shade tree in the Montgomery and Montgomery Law Offices parking lot. He hoped his brother had some news for him about Fitzgerald's place. After ten years of unsuccessfully trying to get Old Man Fitzgerald to sell, Singing Springs Ranch would finally be his. He could feel it in his bones.

He hadn't known Fitzgerald had family, so finding out Caroline Graham was his great-niece was a tad of a surprise, but no big deal. Other than Caroline, no other Fitzgerald family members mentioned in the obit lived here. He couldn't imagine that old tightwad leaving his ranch to any of them. And even if he did, there was no way anyone would up and move to Texas just because they inherited a rundown ranch, especially if that person knew nothing about ranching. Yup. Whoever ended up with Singing Springs would be thrilled to unload it, and Travis wanted to make sure that person unloaded it right into his hands.

He let himself in the back door of his brother's office, stopping long enough to grab a bottle of cold water from the kitchen, then headed for the reception area.

After removing his beige straw cowboy hat, he leaned over the reception desk to give Jason's secretary a wink. "Hi, Mags. Is little brother available?"

"Hey, handsome," Margaret said then sighed. "If only I were twenty years younger and not married…"

Travis slapped his hat across his heart. "My bachelor days would be over."

She smiled and nodded toward the closed door

down the hall. "He's on the phone. I'll let him know you're here. I'd offer you something to drink, but you seemed to have helped yourself."

He rolled the dewy bottle on the back of his neck. "Can't decide if I want to drink this or pour it over my head. Man, it's a killer out there. What about KC? Is my lovely cousin around?"

Before Margaret could respond, Jason's door opened. "I thought I heard a reprobate out here. Stop flirting with my secretary and c'mon back. I've got a date with Lydia tonight and you know she hates when I'm late." He ducked back into his office, leaving the door ajar.

Travis groaned. "I'm coming." He looked at Margaret and hitched his thumb toward the door where his brother had just been standing. "He been in this bad mood all day?"

She shook her head. "Nope. He was quite pleasant when KC headed out about thirty minutes ago. Your cousin's got perfect timing. She always knows to clear out and avoid the Montgomery brothers when something's brewing."

"Lucky me. Wish I knew her magic."

Travis entered his brother's office and closed the door behind him. He dropped onto the thick leather sofa running along the office wall then set his hat crown-side down on the cushion beside him. He draped his arm along the back of the sofa. "I hope you've got some good news for me. I've had a bitch of a day."

"What happened?"

"One of the Webster kids spooked a new stallion I'd just unloaded. The bastard almost trampled me, John and a couple of hands before we could get him under control."

Jason frowned. "I'd think your foreman's kids would know better than to get near a stallion, especially one I suspect was antsy to begin with. Which kid?"

Travis's mouth cocked up on one side in a grimace. "Rocky. He had a classmate visiting, and I think he was trying to impress him. But after John and Nadine get done with him, I suspect his ears will be ringing for the next week." He gave a small chuckle. "And I'm getting my stalls mucked out for free for at least a month, maybe two."

"I hated mucking stalls."

"So I remember. What's the good news?"

Jason took a seat closer to the sofa. "Well, I've got good news and bad news."

"Great. Bad news first then."

"Fitzgerald had KC prepare his will about a year ago, so his estate won't be going to the state to resolve."

Travis scowled. "I was afraid of that," he growled. "So what can you tell me now?"

"All the beneficiaries have been notified and the will duly probated. It was fairly straight forward. I don't foresee anyone challenging it."

"So don't keep me waiting. Who do I need to talk to about buying Singing Springs?"

"Dr. Caroline Graham."

TEXAS FANDANGO

WHISPERING SPRINGS, TEXAS BOOK 3 © 2014
CYNTHIA D'ALBA

Two-weeks on the beach can deepened more than tans.

Attorney KC Montgomery has loved family friend Drake Gentry forever, but she never seemed to be on his radar. When Drake's girlfriend dumps him, leaving him with two all-expenses paid tickets to the Sand Castle Resort in the Caribbean, KC seizes the chance and makes him an offer impossible to refuse: two weeks of food, fun, sand, and sex with no strings attached.

University Professor Drake Gentry has noticed his best friend's cousin for years, but KC has always been hands-off, until today. Unable to resist, he agrees to her two-week, no-strings affair.

The vacation more than fulfills both their fantasies. The sun is hot but the sex hotter.

TEXAS BOSSA NOVA

WHISPERING SPRINGS, TEXAS BOOK 5 ©2014
CYNTHIA D'ALBA

A heavy snowstorm can produce a lot of heat

Magda Hobbs loves being a ranch housekeeper. The job keeps her close to her recently discovered father, foreman at the same ranch. She is immune to all the cowboy charms, except for one certain cowboy, who is wreaking havoc on her libido.

Reno Montgomery is determined to make his fledging cattle ranch a success. Dates with Magda Hobbs rocks his world and then she disappears, leaving him confused and angry. He's shocked when he learns the new live-in housekeeper is Magda Hobbs.

When a freak snowstorm cuts off the outside world, the isolation rekindles their desire. But when the weather and the roads clear, Reno has to work hard and fast to keep the woman of his dreams from hitting the road right out of his life again.

TEXAS HUSTLE

WHISPERING SPRINGS, TEXAS BOOK 6 ©2015
CYNTHIA D'ALBA

Watch out for chigger bites, love bites and secrets that bite

Born into a wealthy, Southern family, Porchia Summers builds a good life in Texas until a bad news ex-boyfriend tracks her down. Desperate for time to figure out how to handle the trouble he brings, she looks to the one man who can get her out of town for a few days.

Darren Montgomery has had his eye on the town's sexy, sweet baker for a while but she's never returns his looks until now. He's flattered but suspicious about her quick change in attention.

Sometimes, camping isn't just camping. It's survival.

TEXAS LULLABY

WHISPERING SPRINGS, TEXAS BOOK 7 ©2016
CYNTHIA D'ALBA

Sometimes what you think you don't want is exactly what you need.

After a long four-year engagement, Lydia Henson makes her decision. Forced to choice between having a family or marrying a man who adamantly against fathering children, she chooses the man. She can live without children. She can't live without the man she loves.

Jason Montgomery doesn't want a family, or at least that's his story and he's sticking to it. The falsehood is less emasculating than the truth.

On the eve of their wedding, Jason and Lydia's well-planned life is thrown into chaos. Everything Jason has sworn he doesn't want is within his grasp. But as he reaches for the golden ring, life delivers another twist.

SADDLES AND SOOT

WHISPERING SPRINGS, TEXAS BOOK 8 ©2015
CYNTHIA D'ALBA

Veterinarian Georgina Greyson will only be in Whispering Springs for three months. She isn't looking for love or roots, but some fun with a hunky fireman could help pass the time.

Tanner Marshall loves being a volunteer fireman, maybe more than being a cowboy. At thirty-four, he's ready to put down some roots, including marriage, children and the white picket fence.

When Georgina accidentally sets her yard on fire during a burn ban, the volunteer fire department responds. Tanner hates carelessness with fire, but there's something about his latest firebug that he can't get out of his mind.

Can an uptight firefighter looking to settle down persuade a cute firebug to give up the road for a house and roots?

TEXAS DAZE

WHISPERING SPRINGS, TEXAS BOOK 9 ©2017
CYNTHIA D'ALBA

A quick fling can sure heat up a cowgirl's life

When a devastating discovery ends Marti Jenkins' engagement, she decides to play the field for a while. A ranch accident lands her in the office of Whispering Springs' new orthopedic doctor, Dr. Eli Boone. And yeah, he's as hot as she's been told.

Dr. Eli Boone is temporarily covering his friend's practice and then it's back to New York City and the societal world he's lives. He's not looking for a wife, but he wouldn't say no to a quick tumble in the sheets with the right woman.

Due to ridiculous challenge, Eli has to learn to ride before he leaves town. He turns to the one person who can help him win the bet, Marti Jenkins.

As he learns to ride a horse, Marti does a little riding of her own…and she doesn't need a horse.

Made in the USA
Coppell, TX
24 January 2021

48738312R00164